By Susan Cheever

LOOKING FOR WORK
A HANDSOME MAN

Susan Cheever

A HANDSOME MAN

SIMON AND SCHUSTER

NEW YORK

Copyright © 1981 by Susan Cheever
All rights reserved
including the right of reproduction
in whole or in part in any form
Published by Simon and Schuster
A Division of Gulf & Western Corporation
Simon & Schuster Building
Rockefeller Center
1230 Avenue of the Americas
New York, New York 10020
SIMON AND SCHUSTER and colophon are trademarks of Simon & Schuster

Designed by Eve Kirch
Manufactured in the United States of America

1   2   3   4   5   6   7   8   9   10

Library of Congress Cataloging in Publication Data

Cheever, Susan.
A handsome man.
I. Title.
PS3553.H3487H3   813'.54   80-27179

ISBN 0-671-42395-9

To Susan Colgan

Chapter

1

Hannah Bart looked out through the double thickness of plastic at dawn over the Atlantic. Pink rim of the horizon, fleecy soft floor of clouds. In the next seat a fat man read and reread a mimeographed sheet of tour instructions, whispering each word to himself below the steady whine of the engine. His shiny sleeve usurped the plastic armrest between their places. He was probably about Sam's age, but that was certainly all they had in common. *Bring a rain hat,* the instructions said. Five hours out of Kennedy his wife took a white vinyl bonnet out of her flight bag, set it on her head, and tied it securely under her chin. I'm not like that, Hannah thought, at least I'm not like that.

As the plane started to descend, she climbed out over the couple's double-knit knees and into the aisle. The passengers behind her slumped in their places with their mouths hanging open in uncomfortable sleep. A pair of horn-rimmed glasses had fallen into her path and she carefully placed them next to their snoring, slack-jawed owner. He responded with a grunt, and turned over in his dreams, knocking the glasses off to the floor on the other side out of her reach. Both of the tiny lavatories at the end of the aisle were vacant. She locked herself in one of them and rested her carry-on canvas bag on the toilet. Bracing herself against the door, she took off her flowered summer dress and changed into the skirt, silk shirt and boots folded in the bag. Crumpled paper towels littered the counter and a cake of green soap melted in a small puddle on the metal sink.

Hannah brought her face close to the mirror, holding the edge of the sink to steady herself against the vibration of the plane. Not too bad. Brown eyes clear, blond highlights okay, skin tight, hair fluffed out around her round face, stomach pretty flat—although a small roll of flesh puffed out above the waistband of the skirt. Clean living. No sweets, no sex, no staying out late and getting bombed on white wine and nursing a hangover through the next day at work on doughnuts and brackish coffee from the Lexington Avenue Delicatessen.

There had been moments of panic, times when she was overwhelmed with sharp loneliness for Sam, and other times when she woke up terrified about what she had gotten herself into. But she had stayed in control. She had not lined up a lot of other men, just-in-case men, and she had dulled her anxiety with exercise. Had Sam been as celibate? Probably not, even though he ought to be more nervous than she was. He had other ways of dealing with fear. Glossier ways. But that wasn't going to bother her this time. This time she was going to be above petty jealousy and immune to anxiety attacks. She was going to concentrate on the important things.

"I am going to be magnificent," she told herself out loud, grinning at her reflection in the smeared mirror. "I am going to be absolutely magnificent."

A tinny female voice from somewhere above her broke into

8

her personal tête-à-tête. "Please fasten your seatbelts for our descent into Shannon Airport," it said. "The Captain has turned on the No-Smoking sign."

Hannah stubbed out the cigarette she had propped on the sink under the No-Smoking-in-the-Lavatory sign, shouldered her bag, flushed the blue swirl of disinfectant down the toilet bowl, and opened the door to the cabin. Her seatmates grumbled and clucked in irritation as she maneuvered back to the window at the last minute, trying not to wrinkle her new skirt or touch their inert, terrified bodies.

She was afraid, too, in spite of herself. Especially during takeoffs and landings. Her brother Jake was always telling her that she was safer in a commercial jet than she was in her own car on the Saw Mill River Parkway. Jake was always reciting the statistics, but she didn't care, it didn't *feel* as safe. She couldn't keep her mind off what it would be like if something went wrong—a clogged fuel line, a hairline crack along a pylon, a bolt slowly losing hold—and what it would be like in those quick seconds when she knew that she was going to die. She tightened her seatbelt buckle and dug her fingernails into her palms. *Our Father who art in heaven, hallowed be thy name.* The plane creaked and trembled as the landing gear was lowered, and the black asphalt of the runway rose suddenly up through the mist toward her window. Not too fast, please not too fast. *Thy Kingdom come, thy will be done,* she started again, straining to locate an image in her mind that she could think of as God. Please don't let me die right now.

The wheels bumped down, skidded, and bumped again. The plane seemed to be straining to hold together as the giant engines went into reverse. As the cabin shook and a great roar drowned out her thoughts, she began to relax.

The danger was over.

Hannah had always wanted to be the kind of passenger

9

who acted as if nothing unusual had happened when the plane landed. That kind of person finished what they were reading, got up and stretched, put on their coat in their own good time, and strolled out of the cabin looking relaxed and confident. But she couldn't wait. She pushed to the head of the line as usual, bumping the people behind her and jostling the stewardess as she shifted her canvas bag to squeeze into her raincoat.

Finally the cabin door was opened and she caught the soft damp smell of Irish morning. Grass and sweet dew mixed with the stale air of the plane after a long flight. As she walked through a tunnel to the customs area her heart began to pound. Two officials in dark-blue uniforms waved passengers through the baggage inspection aisles and she lined up to have her passport stamped at a glass booth.

"Welcome to Ireland. I hope you have good weather," the man said as he banged a rubber stamp down on the page, and she smiled back at him. Her mouth filled with cotton. A bead of sweat trickled down her side under the silk shirt. Sam would be there, she reassured herself. Sam was always on time—he didn't need to be late. She picked up her suitcase, shouldered the canvas bag, and walked down the corridor to the airport waiting room.

Her eyes searched the blur of anxious, expectant faces at the exit gate. He wasn't there, of course not. He was standing on the other side of the room, away from the crowd, a tall man in corduroys leaning calmly against the wall under a map of Ireland, reading the *Irish Times*. He lowered the newspaper and caught her eye. She smiled as he walked toward her. He was wearing a new sweater. His hair was longer and it curled softly above the turned-up collar of his tweed jacket.

"Hi, kiddo," he said.

"Hi."

Sam didn't make a fuss, he didn't like fuss. But she could

tell that he was glad to see her. He would take care of her now. He picked up her bag, kissed her lightly on both cheeks, and gently took her elbow with his free hand to guide her out through the glass doors of the airport.

With her parents, and with her ex-husband, Joe, Hannah had driven around Europe in a succession of fly-drive package-tour cars of the sub-compact variety. Ford Escorts, Renault Fives, Seats and Fiat 600s. Sam's rented car was a white Alfa Romeo convertible, and instead of obediently parking it in a distant airport parking lot he had brought it right up to the curb of the arrivals building. No one questioned his right to be there. As he moved with assurance around the car to swing open the trunk, she felt a pleasing jolt of recognition. What a handsome man! What a glamorous man! Sam radiated a kind of polish and ease that her memory never did justice to. When she was with him, it always surprised her.

At first, of course, she had distrusted it—and him. Last fall, when they had started, when he had called her after they ran into each other on Madison Avenue that time, she had thought he was a little too good to be true. She had heard about Sam Noble, she had even read about Sam Noble in Liz Smith and *Women's Wear Daily*. How could you take anything seriously with a man like that? She laughed when he sent her roses after their first night together. It was fun being with him, because she hoped for nothing. He was the president of his own classy publishing house, after all, and she was a flack in the publicity department of Barter Books, and she wasn't about to forget it, even if he pretended to. She was too savvy to lose her balance over someone like that.

"What makes you think he's not serious about you?" the psychiatrist said. She rocked back in her vinyl office chair, her pen poised above a spiral notebook with Hannah's name on it.

"He's not the serious type," Hannah said.

"You should have more self-confidence." She looked up at Hannah's skeptical expression. *"You know that?"*

"I know that."

Now she watched as Sam closed the trunk of the car. The metal shut with a satisfying, expensive-sounding *clunk*.

"Nice car," Hannah said, trying not to sound impressed.

"Only a fitting chariot for the fairest lass in Ireland," Sam said, shortening the vowels and rolling his r's in a mock Irish brogue.

That's just the way it always was with Sam. He was elaborately polite and chivalrous, but he often seemed to be making fun of his own behavior at the same time. It didn't matter. His imitation of a gentleman and a troubadour was a lot more pleasant than the bumbling excuses and alarming demands of men her own age. It had taken her a while to get used to it, though. When she first started meeting Sam's friends, going to their parties in sleek East Side apartments and ending up afterward at Elaine's, they had made her feel like a clumsy adolescent. Slender women with high cheekbones and low voices. Famous writers in tweeds.

But she had spent some more money on clothes and braved the chilly receptionists at Elizabeth Arden and Kenneth and after a while Sam and Sam's set seemed a little less intimidating. They were friendly enough—if only because she was with Sam. She had started smoking again too. It made her feel less nervous; it gave her something to do with her hands. And Sam made smoking seem so glamorous with the way he offered his special Dunhill cigarettes from the monogrammed case and then bent over to light them, sheltering that intimate moment with his long fingers, the flash of his signet ring and the woman's expectant face lit for a moment by the flame.

Now a light rain began to fall, covering the windshield with watery lace. The asphalt shimmered as Sam turned the car north, following the curving ramps out of the airport.

"Where are we going?"

"A place called Ballymarr."

"Is that a town?"

"No, it's near a town, though—Letterkenny," Sam said. "Ballymarr is a hotel in one of the old castles at the northern end of the island. It'll take us a couple of days to get there so I've made reservations in Galway and Donegal. Donegal's a little grim, but we won't be there long. Does that suit you?"

"Galway, Donegal." She curled down in the soft leather passenger seat, feeling happy. "I love those Irish names."

Sam was quiet for a minute as he turned the car out onto a bigger road. "I called Travis from London and he's planning to get up there sometime next week," he said. "That will give us a few days to settle in before he arrives."

Hannah's coziness evaporated. Now that they were on the four-lane highway, she noticed with a panicky start that they were speeding down the wrong side of the road. Of course. Just like England. She felt strangely vulnerable and disoriented as Sam stepped on the gas to maneuver the car past a dilapidated Morris Mini.

"Have you been to the hotel before?" she asked.

"No, I've heard high recommendations of it, though. It's supposed to have wonderful trout fishing. I brought my rods and there's an old one my mother used that I thought would be right for you. It's hard to find a bamboo rod like that these days. Have you ever fished for trout?"

"No, I guess I haven't."

"I think you'll like it," Sam said. "When we get up there I can give you some casting lessons."

"Is it hard?"

13

Sam smiled. "Not too hard for the finest mind at Barter Books," he said.

The road narrowed to two lanes again and the car hissed down the rainy pavement, past alleys of great plane trees and through pale groves of beech, by the ruins of ancient manor houses and between rows of roofless, collapsing stone huts. The country looked strangely empty and deserted. Farmers had once lived and grown their crops and raised their families in those huts, and lords and ladies had ruled from the manor houses: where had they all gone? In a way, the flatness of the land reminded her of her childhood and home, the prairie and the big Illinois sky with the distant glow from the lights of Chicago off behind the water towers at night.

There was an eerie familiarity about Ireland. Images from James Joyce and Yeats and O'Casey floated by the car windows in the light rain. A village priest in his black beret and vestments bicycled down a dirt lane on his way to Mass. Two whiskey-faced farmers blocked a side road with a cart and a shaggy black-and-white pony. There were the bright red hair and freckled faces from the children in *Dubliners,* and the wide eyes of Christy Mahon in *The Playboy of the Western World.*

At Clarecastle Sam slowed the car down to pass through the village main street, and she watched a gang of Irish schoolboys in short gray-flannel pants and blue uniform jackets laughing and pushing each other on the way home for lunchtime:

Stephen Dedalus is my name,
Ireland is my nation.
Clongowes is my dwellingplace
And Heaven my expectation.

14

Sam pulled the car off the road outside a pub near Crusheen at about noon. She suddenly felt very hungry although she knew it was just dawn in New York and her stomach was playing tricks on her. The thatched roof of the pub beetle-browed over pale-green stucco walls, and a faded portrait of a boar swung from two creaking hinges above the door.

"Good, I'm ready for lunch," she said. She watched from the warm refuge of a huge leather chair in front of the peat fire as Sam ordered two Guinnesses and waited for the publican to make fresh sandwiches. Sam had a way of making decisions for anyone who was with him, of announcing which restaurant they should go to, and ordering for them when they got there. Sometimes this was irritating, but now she was grateful for it. She watched as he stood in the dim light at the bar, leaning on his elbow and talking with the bartender about the fishing and the weather as if he'd known him for years. In an old lithograph above the smoke-stained wooden mantelpiece a crowd of men in red coats, on horseback, chased an orange fox through a rocky field.

After lunch the warmth of the dark beer and the food and the rhythm of the moving car made her drowsy. The landscape's greenness calmed her and the rain made a soothing *swish* against the tires. Sam was taking care of her. She imagined herself at home in New York, snuggled under her down comforter, with the dappled light of early morning coming in through the blinds, and she drifted in and out of a contented doze.

When she woke up they were coming into Galway, through narrow streets lined with gray stone Georgian facades. The rain had stopped. The road went out to a seawall and Sam slowed down as they passed rows of pastel stucco houses, blue and green and beige, standing at the edge of the bay. The fishing fleet croodled against a long cement pier with its nets hung out to dry, battered wooden trawlers, creaking and clanking with the tide. *Star Immaculate. Roving Swan. Our Lady of the Waves.* Sam swung the car around a sharp corner away from the sea, past a massive brick railroad station, and drove into a big central square. It was once Eyre Square, she saw from the map, but its name had been changed. It was now John F. Kennedy Square. Sam drew up in front of the forbidding stone monument which dominated one end of it, and a man in livery and white gloves stepped out of the shadows of the interior to meet them.

It was a grand hotel in the old style of Grand Hotels. They followed the bellboy up the huge steps and into a cavernous main lobby, and he led them to their room through a labyrinth of long, dark, high-ceilinged halls. The room itself, and the whole building, looked as if it had been built for a race of giants. A double bed that could comfortably sleep five took up one wall opposite a huge bureau with an enormous mirror perched on Victorian wooden brackets on top of it. Hannah felt like a dwarf as she opened the vast wardrobes and drawers and unpacked her pathetic-looking piles of clothing. In the mirror on the bureau she could just see the top half of her head. Even Sam looked small, sitting on one of the gigantic carved-wood and cut-velvet *fauteuils* that flanked the bureau.

By the time they had finished unpacking, she was starving again. It was past lunchtime in New York. She began to feel light-headed and cranky. Distant smells of food cooking in the hotel kitchens wafted down the halls and under their door. Sam had unpacked his guidebook and he was reading about Galway. It was the Noble family guidebook and its red leather covers looked worn out.

"Isn't that a little out of date?" she said.

"Nothing ever changes in Ireland."

16

"Well, what does it say about food?"

Sam closed the book and led her downstairs. "Let's have a drink first, it's early," he said. In spite of her longing glances in what she imagined was the direction of the dining room, he took her arm firmly and walked back out through the lobbies and into town and down a narrow lane toward the sea. Why didn't she just assert herself? Why didn't she just come right out and say that she was tired and hungry, and that she would just as soon eat at the hotel? If she did, she knew that Sam would be exquisitely polite about it, as he was about everything.

"Of course, what a nice idea," he would say, although she would know that he had made other plans and that he was abandoning them. "Why didn't I think of it? You must be very tired." But she kept silent. It was usually a bad idea to say what you wanted, especially with a man like Sam. If you asked for what you wanted and you didn't get it, that was disappointing and embarrassing. If you asked for what you wanted and you did get it, then you were exposed, and vulnerable, and in debt to whoever had given it to you.

They walked through the big square and down to the seawall that stretched along the harbor's edge. With his arm around her shoulders, Sam guided her toward a brick house on the water side of the street. Inside a small room, a dozen places were set with white linen and silver and wineglasses, and a friendly young man in a blue turtleneck led them to a table by the window. Outside, she could see the twilight on the stillness of the evening sea and the fishing boats creaking at anchor. She ordered lobster and the waiter brought it out for her to see, alive and still bursting with its black, succulent roe. A sauceboat of pale melted butter came with her dinner and, concentrating totally, she began sucking the tart, salty ocean juices out of the smaller claws and dipping the rich lobster meat into butter and lemon and scooping out the deep red roe and green tomalley from the creature's inner cavities.

"Sam," she said, "how come you always know exactly what I want, even when I don't?"

"Practice." He smiled at her buttery face and lifted the last of the Pouilly-Fumé out of its icy silver bucket. "Fifty years of practice."

It was practice too, and age, and Sam's politeness, that kept him from rushing her, from pawing her in the car or leaping on her in the hotel room, or hustling her off to bed as another man might have. Sam was even polite about sex. He was ready when she was. It bothered her. Sometimes she wished he was a little less cool and in control in hot, intimate moments. And a little less controllable. When they made love, she often excited herself by imagining a rougher man. A man who would tell her what to do and leave her no choices, a man who would allow her to play at resisting him —for a while. She craved the urgency of the first time, each first time, the riotous tingling of a stranger's touch, the race of the blood, and the incomparable moment of surrender. On the floor of the living room, in the office chair, between the sheets of an unfamiliar bed.

"How many men have you slept with since you were divorced from Joe?" the psychiatrist asked. Her head was bent over the notepad, Hannah couldn't see her eyes as she answered.

"Don't you think that's a little high?"

Tonight was different. She was tired and longed for gentleness. Nothing could have fitted her mood better than Sam's precise caresses and his well-mannered lovemaking. And afterward she was happy to fall asleep at last, her body curled spoon-fashion against his back in the cozy trough of the mattress.

Chapter

2

She woke up slowly to the sound of Sam's morning rituals. The *clip, clip, clip* of the silver scissors from his manicure case as he trimmed his nails. The five splashes as he finished shaving in the basin on the other side of the bathroom wall. The rhythmic slapping sound of his ivory-handled shaving brush as he knocked it back and forth against the door frame to get the water out. Through two sets of drapes framing high, high windows, she saw the flat gray morning sky and she remembered that they were in Ireland.

For a moment, as the familiar sounds filtered through layers of sleep, she had thought they were back in Sam's apartment, and her heart had lifted happily as it always did when she woke up there. Sam Noble's apartment. Sam's place, with its marble floors and its inherited furniture and the baby grand in the living room. Sam's rooms were so perfectly furnished, so complete, so finished off, that they sometimes made her feel like a mischievous child visiting grandparents. Once, when she had taken over the kitchen to make pancakes on Sunday morning, Sam's cook had even complained to him about the flour being put back in the wrong cupboard. The bed, with its dust ruffle and matching spread and bolsters, made her feel like bouncing on it. And she often stifled the impulse to relax with her feet up on the mahogany butler's table in front of the velvet couch in the living room. Sam pretended not to mind her manners, or her teasing, but he *had* been careful to warn her that the table's brass hinges were weak. And he often laid a coaster out invitingly near where she might be tempted to put a wet glass on the shimmering veneer of the end tables.

When Sam was busy, she had devoted herself to exploring every inch of his apartment with delight and curiosity. It was only ten blocks away from the comfortable jumble of her own rooms, but it was another world. At Sam's everything was always in place. His shirts and socks and underwear were freshly laundered and neatly folded in the appropriate drawers. His shoes were shined and ready on a long rack in the closet, each pair with its own wooden shoe trees. His suit for the next day hung over a wooden valet, and his brushes were always just so on the glass surface of the table in the big bathroom. (He had taken down the wall between the bathroom and the dressing room to make it larger.) Sam had owned the apartment for a long time, he told her, but he had only moved in completely two years ago, when his divorce came through. It was hard to believe that it hadn't been exactly as it was forever.

Her most rewarding explorations were in Sam's library, where all the books were carefully shelved in alphabetical order. There were the book prizes Sam had won for his essays at St. Paul's and later at Williams, and his grandfather's sets of Proust and Dickens with their soft maroon leather covers and their elaborate old-fashioned bookplates. *Ex Libris* Samuel Adams Noble. There were no paperbacks in Sam's library.

20

In the cupboards below the bookshelves she found the Noble family photograph albums. There was a row of smaller books, bound in red leather, with pages filled with old sepia-tinted photographs in ink-drawn frames. They were portraits of people long ago, women in bustles and men in straw boaters, rowing boats and standing beneath trees on summer afternoons. Two larger albums, bound in blue leather, were the ones that fascinated Hannah. They began with Sam's baby pictures, interspersed with the documents and paraphernalia of his life. His birth certificate, his first four-leaf clover, his report card from The Buckley School. There were pictures of Sam as a young man, looking smoother and slighter than he did now. Sam in baggy white flannels, standing on the tennis courts at East Hampton before the war, and Sam clowning around on graduation day with his mortarboard rakishly cocked over one eye. A group of three formal-looking portraits showed Sam in the Navy, looking much too young and unsure for his blue officer's cap and the ribbons on his uniform.

The second album began with wedding pictures. There was Sam in a frock coat, still looking too young to be there, dancing with Nancy in her tiers of white lace. In another picture they stood at the wedding reception, framed by the fat white doric columns of the Belle Haven Club. There were honeymoon pictures of Europe: Nancy looking blond and stiff as she sat at a table at the Café de Flore in Paris (taken by Sam), and Sam gazing pensively into the distance as they made the crossing from Calais on the Dover boat (taken by Nancy). Then there was a picture of Nancy in a flowered dress, sitting on the grass in some summer place and looking very pregnant. And then lots of pictures of another baby, Travis—Hannah wondered why he didn't have his own book —and another little boy growing up.

There was Travis at his first birthday party, smiling and

gurgling in front of a huge cake with one candle. And Travis as a little boy in a sailor suit, perched ecstatically on his father's shoulders. There was an eighth-grade graduation picture of Travis standing in the back row of boys at the Ashmont Country Day School, and on the next page a picture of Travis in track shorts and a shirt with the number 1 on it, posing before a race. But that was all. The last half of the book was blank, with a few odd photographs stuck haphazardly between the pages. From the dates and captions on the pictures, she figured out that Travis must be about nineteen or twenty now. What had happened to him? Sam never mentioned him, or Nancy, and the disorganization at the end of the album was so odd and out of place in Sam's well-ordered life that something must have gone terribly wrong. For a long time she was afraid to ask about it.

Hannah was very close to her own family. She called home at least once a week, and she and her brother Jake usually spent their summers there, swimming in the lake and playing tennis and falling in and out of love with the people they grew up with. She did this a lot more than Jake, of course; he was ten years younger and not so mischievous. He tended to take everything very, very seriously and he had a habit of backing up most of his arguments with esoteric statistics or quotes from Pliny the elder or Pitt the younger. But he was a good listener and in many ways her closest friend.

Her father had been a professor at the university for as long as she could remember, and her mother had always seemed perfectly happy in the role life had given her, academic wife and suburban mother. They were a happy family, a family of four friends, and she often leaned on them in her mind. It was fun to talk about them, of course, and she noticed that Sam seemed to like hearing about them. She would begin by apologizing for their ordinariness, and end up making him laugh with her over some silly incident or prank from her childhood. It was after one of these talks that she asked about Travis.

"Where's Travis? I mean, what happened to him?" she asked.

Sam stopped laughing and looked out the window. They were sitting in the living room. He put his drink down and folded his legs, resting his ankle on his knee and bending over slightly toward the butler's table.

"I'm afraid he's out in Colorado somewhere," he said.

"Do you ever see him?"

"No, not for a long time." Sam's face looked pinched and unhappy. His jaw muscles clenched and unclenched under the skin.

"Listen, maybe you don't want to talk about it," she said.

"It's not that."

"What's the trouble, then?"

Slowly, answering her questions, Sam told her about Travis. And about why the subject upset him. His son had always been a wonderful, charming, and difficult child, Sam explained. Everyone loved Travis. But as an adolescent, about the time he had gone off to boarding school, he had become impossible to deal with. Sam had lost touch with him somehow, and Travis was so rebellious and angry that sometimes Sam was amazed that they were father and son.

At St. Paul's, where Sam had been the best quarterback in a decade and president of the student body, Travis's bad attitude and general disobedience had gotten him expelled —even though he was the only third-former to make the varsity track team. Sam got him into Southfield—the head-master was an old classmate of his from Williams, and Travis's athletic ability helped—but after a year there he was in serious trouble again. There was something disruptive about Travis at school. His grades were bad. When he broke

23

the rules it made other boys want to break the rules, too. At Bristol Academy it was the same story. Travis dropped back a grade to take off the academic pressure, but nothing helped. It was the first time Bristol had been able to compete against the Exeter track team, but even that didn't outweigh the trouble he caused. He was way behind in all his classes anyway, and he didn't even seem to care. Sam drove up to Bristol and brought him back to Ashmont in disgrace. He enrolled Travis in Ashmont High School, but during the summer he hitchhiked out west for a summer job and never came back.

Sometimes Travis wrote his mother, and Nancy sent the letters on to Sam. That was the only communication they had. Sam knew that he had worked pumping gas in Glenwood Springs, joined the Aspen Highlands ski patrol for a while, and was now a hand on a sheep ranch in Carbondale. As Sam talked he leaned against her on the couch and curled his body as if he had an internal ache. She comforted him, stroking his back.

"Don't feel bad about it, it sounds as if you did everything you could," she said. She concentrated on sounding reassuring, although she didn't think Sam had done everything he could at all. If Travis had been her son or her brother, she would never, ever have let him go like that.

"I'm not so sure," Sam said, speaking into the sleeve of her sweater.

"Well, maybe you should try to see him now, maybe you could get along with him now."

Sam straightened up. His old self. "I don't think you really understand what's involved," he said. "Would you like a drink?" And they dropped the subject.

Sam obviously didn't want to talk about Travis any more, but now she couldn't stop thinking about him. Knowing the story of Travis's decline made her see Sam in a slightly different way. Maybe his control, his perfection, was really a way of avoiding life with its wonderful messes and complications. Sam protected himself with formulas; he was afraid not to. She knew that a son of hers, or a son of her parents, would have had much more attention and support than it sounded like Travis got. They would have at least enrolled him in another school—maybe another kind of school—not one of those uptight paramilitary grooming grounds like St. Paul's, and not a second-rate imitation of one, either.

There was a part of her that couldn't accept Sam's story. He reminded her of Axel Heyst in *Victory* and the way Heyst had avoided his own life by taking his father's advice: "Look on—make no sound." Look on, make no sound, she had hated Heyst for that, and she was glad when Conrad ended the book in violence and a whirlwind of fire. Maybe Sam's relationship with his son was none of her business, but she wasn't going to look on and make no sound. She brought the subject up as often as she dared, although she knew it irritated Sam. Sometimes he was gracious and friendly about it, sometimes he even seemed about to give in to her suggestions that he call Travis, or write him at least. Other times when she brought the conversation around to Travis, he would be stiff and defensive. "Don't you think we've talked about Travis enough?" he would say.

In a way, he was right. They had talked about Travis enough, but Hannah couldn't seem to stop herself. If Sam was so rigid, so inflexible that he couldn't write a letter to his only son, she wanted him to admit it. She wanted to know. Sam had everything, but perhaps he had everything at the price of being close to nothing. Was he, she suggested, too uptight and too middle-aged to change?

The more she persisted, the more annoyed Sam seemed to get. She began to think she might lose him over this. He would cling to his precarious hold on himself, to his daily rituals and his self-serving assumptions about life, even if it meant breaking off with her—the way he had broken off with Travis. Of course, it would all be accomplished with a smoothness and savoir faire that would be meant to leave her wondering what had happened. But she would know.

When he began talking about his biannual business trip to London, her anxiety level soared. Was this his way of ending it? When he got back, he would just forget to call. Of course, she couldn't confront him with this, you could never fight with Sam. He turned away the most provocative remarks with polite incredulity or gentlemanly impatience. "I'm sure you don't mean that, sweetie," he would say.

And summer was coming. Hannah set great store by summer plans, and she didn't have any. Sam was going to London—even Jake was going to Europe as his twenty-first birthday present from her parents—and she was going to be left to sweat through another stinky New York summer with her old boyfriends for company. Poor Hannah. She felt as abandoned as she imagined Travis felt.

"Why don't you take Travis to London with you?" she asked once. "That's what my parents are doing, they're sending Jake abroad. You could all meet up over there. Jake and Travis are about the same age, I think."

"You have some interesting ideas," Sam said. She gave up. It was going to be a long, lonely summer for her, while Jake and Sam and maybe even Travis gallivanted around Europe. Since she was losing Sam anyway, she relaxed. They might as well have a good time in the little time they had left. Of course—wasn't that the way it always was?—as soon as she stopped wanting something to happen, it happened.

It was a Saturday morning in the middle of May. She walked down Fifth Avenue to Sam's apartment to meet him for lunch, and the New York spring air made her head spin with pleasure. The bushes in the park were bursting with fragrant pink and yellow blossoms, and there were tulips in the little iron enclosures around the trees on the sidewalk. Slim women in bright print summer dresses headed out of the Avenue's elegant buildings for the shops on Madison. New York was wonderful, and she belonged here. Maybe when Sam went to London she would take a share in one of the houses in the Hamptons that people at work were teaming up to rent. David would go in with her. She'd get some tan and eat some lobsters and have a quick sun-warmed summer affair. If Sam *did* call her when he got back, she would be happy and busy, very busy.

The lobby of Sam's building was dark and cool after the bright outdoors. She gave the elevator man a dazzling smile —he wouldn't have her to smirk at any more. When she rang Sam's doorbell, the cleaning lady let her in.

"He's in the library," she said.

Hannah's eye was stopped dead by a stack of blue-and-white airline tickets lying on the flat silver dish on the table under the gilt-framed mirror in the hall. She picked up the top ticket and quickly opened the folder. There was Travis's name. She squinted intently at the tiny printed numbers and abbreviations that would tell her the whole story, then she put the ticket carefully back on the dish. She didn't want to get caught being too curious. She walked through the living room, where the sun streamed onto the Oriental carpet and made its colors blaze, and into the library. Sam was sitting at the desk in the dark room, poring over a manuscript under the green shade of the reading lamp.

"Hey, come out of your cave, it's spring!" she said. He looked up at her slowly over his Benjamin Franklin half-glasses.

"Is that so?"

"Listen, are you going to take Travis to Europe after all?"

"What makes you think that, nosy?"

27

"I guess I looked at some airline tickets that happened to be lying on the hall table," she said. "Is that your idea of a hiding place?" How flattering it would be, after all, if he followed her suggestion about Travis. He was listening to her.

"Yes. Travis is going to go to Ireland, and I'll meet him there after London. Do you approve?"

"Definitely."

"That's good, because I thought since it was your idea you might like to come, too."

She looked down at the tooled-leather top of the desk as if she were thinking it over. Playing for time. Naturally she was dying to go. A trip with Sam would be the last word in comfort and elegance. Fun. At the same time, she had made up her mind not to get involved in Sam's problems with Travis. On the other hand, if it was she who reconciled them, neither of them would ever forget her.

A trip to Ireland was a big commitment for Sam. His friends would take her more seriously and her own friends would be impressed. The shrink was right, she should have more self-confidence. David would be furious, though. Oh, I'm afraid I can't go out to Amagansett after all, I'll be spending the summer in Ireland with Sam Noble, tra la. And how could Sam help but love her after that? It was almost like living together. It was a big deal. She wasn't sure that she wanted to live with Sam, but she was sure that she wanted him to want to live with her.

"You're pretty bossy," she said, and she leaned over the desk toward Sam, knocking the manuscript and the fountain pen to the floor as she gave him a hug. "Of course I want to come." Sam returned her kiss and held her gently by the shoulders. At least five minutes passed before he stooped down to regather the manuscript and pick up the pen.

"Why are you attracted to men with these difficulties?" the psychiatrist said. Outside the window it was raining. The weekend spring sunshine had given way to a cold, damp Monday afternoon. She thought about the new raincoat she was planning to buy for the trip. It should be light and chic-looking but kind of classic. Maybe she should have a look in Bloomingdale's on her way home.

"I asked you a question," the psychiatrist said. "This trip sounds as if it will bring up a lot of problems that you may not be ready to deal with. Would you like to come in twice a week for a while?"

"I really don't have time," Hannah said. "What kinds of problems?"

"Well, you seem to have created a situation where you can't possibly get the warmth and attention that you seem to need. Why do you get involved with a man like that? Have you thought that you might be afraid of commitment?"

"No," Hannah said. "He is."

Chapter

3

Tuam, Dunmore, Cloonfad, Ballyhaunis, Charlestown, Collooney. Later, as they drove north from Galway toward Sligo
the land bubbled up into rocky gray hills covered with a
latticework of stone walls. Far off she could see strange square
shapes of the mountains and cliffs closer to the sea. In the
peat bogs that lined the road, men stooped over the earth,
cutting it into rough squares with primitive tools.

At noon Sam turned the car off the main road and headed
for the sea. As they twisted and turned over the rolling hills
she saw patches of the cold, foaming Atlantic in the distance.
Sam pulled over in the tiny parking lot of a brick building
with gleaming white shutters and carefully planted flower
gardens. Geraniums and zinnias and pansies nodded against
a neat picket fence. Over the door a red-and-white-painted
sign said "The Trout," and near the window a wooden placard advertising Guinness was bolted to the bricks.

The pub was in the lee of a grassy ridge which separated
them from the sea. Near the top, the grass gave way to a cliff
streaked with piles of gray talus stone, and above that the
remains of a ruined stone building jutted abruptly out into
the blue sky.

30

"I've got a terrific idea," she said.

"Me too. Go right into this pub and have a nice lunch."

"Oh, come on, Sam, we're on vacation. Couldn't we just change into sneakers and climb up there? It looks so beautiful."

"It's a long way."

"Probably not as bad as it looks from here."

"Well, we're already sort of late," he said.

"Late for a hotel? Come on, please, it'll be fun."

"All right, sweetie, if that's what your heart desires, let's go," he said, opening the trunk to get their shoes.

She could feel the gentlemanly edge. Sam was being polite about it. He wasn't going to make a fuss even if it meant giving in to girlish whims and missing lunch and being late and probably ruining their whole schedule. The steely blade of his good manners infuriated her sometimes. What a tyrant! What a stick-in-the-mud! With Sam, even holidays had to be planned. He always had reservations. He was always on time. His whole life had been a perfect, compulsive plan. He had stayed married for twenty years because marriage was part of his plan. (Hannah hadn't stayed married a moment longer than was absolutely necessary.) Nancy had lived in the big house in Ashmont and brought up Travis. Sam kept his New York apartment and went out to the suburbs on weekends. That was the plan. Once they had had a marriage. Then they had an "arrangement." Now they were divorced. So much for planning.

They changed in silence. Sam laced up his boots with the rubber bottoms and leather uppers, while she slipped on her sneakers and a loose pair of jeans from the suitcase, screening her body behind the car as she dressed. Sam locked the car and followed her up the gradual slope at the bottom. They walked to an abandoned stone farmhouse on an overgrown dirt road and started on a narrow path toward the cliff.

As they climbed, Hannah realized that she had miscalculated the distance from the car. The path was longer and steeper than it looked. The ground was spongy and wet, and what had seemed to be a meadow with good firm footing turned out to be a patch of high clumps of moss, protruding at crazy angles from a slippery bog. Her heart beat loudly against the cage of her chest and blood flowed to her face. Water seeped insidiously through the canvas tops of her shoes. The pub would have been warm and dry, Guinness and smoked salmon sandwiches. Vacations were for relaxing. Sam was right.

At the base of the cliff the path ended, and she began the scramble upward, using her hands to steady herself against the rock. Loose shale and pebbles and small boulders went bounding down the hillside beneath her. Sweat dripped down the sides of her face, but when she stopped to look back at Sam, climbing courteously behind her, he seemed as cool, crisp, and in command as ever.

"Maybe this wasn't such a good idea," she panted.

"Would you like to stop and rest for a minute?" he asked. This sent her stumbling up the last part of the rise with renewed energy.

But at the top, the view suddenly opened out before them like the curtain going up at the opera. The worn foundations of an ancient chapel, blown by the wind and weather into a haunted, holy shape, stood out above the long, sheer drop to the sea on the other side. Streaks of salty white lather blew off the crests of the great blue ocean swells, and the sea foamed around a few bleak rocky islets that poked out of the water offshore. Below them, the wild dance of the waves crashed against the cliff, sending up great plumes of spray.

On the calm side of the ridge, peaceful velvety-green fields sloped down to a sheltered harbor where a fishing boat chugged serenely home. Cows grazed near the doll-house shape of the abandoned farmhouse they had passed, and the white spot of the car flashed in the sun next to the pub.

Sam put his arms around her and sweetly kissed the back of her sweaty neck. "Look at what I would miss without you to push me into things," he said.

"A lot of steep climbing over uncertain terrain when you could be having a beer in a nice warm pub," she said. I love you, she thought. Take care of me.

"There are more important things than beer," he said. "I think."

They started down. Now her legs ached and the wind chilled her through damp clothes. Slowly she stepped and slid down the steep, treacherous cliff with Sam next to her for support. The clumps of grass seemed higher, and the bog sucked at her clammy shoes. The car seemed to stay stubbornly in the distance.

Just above the farmhouse she began to relax. They had made it. As she straightened up to a more normal walk, her foot caught on one of the grassy clumps and she lost her balance. Throwing out her right arm to break her fall, she hit her wrist against a rock and she heard the grinding clink and crunch of glass on stone as her watch smashed against it. She saw the sunlight catch for a moment in the web of crystal splinters, and then the whole watch face fell out of its frame and into pieces on the ground. Her heart sank and she felt sad. It was the watch her father had given her when she went to New York to look for work. The helpless, jagged pieces of it upset her. She was suddenly tired and homesick and she felt like crying. Her family was so far away. She was so far away from home.

Sam knelt down next to her where she lay on the wet ground, and he unfastened the sad, bent circlet of gold from her wrist. He put the watch carefully in the pocket of his corduroy pants. Then he took off his own watch and buckled it onto her.

33

"Come on, then," he said, taking her head in both his hands so gently. "We'll see if we can't get that fixed. Don't be sad, it's okay, it will be all right."

Sam's watch was an object of great beauty. It was of an old Cartier design and he had inherited it from his father, or his father's father. She had often admired its flat golden face and buttery-soft leather strap. But now, as she turned her wrist this way and that to watch the light reflect off its beveled surfaces, the watch made her uncomfortable. Her sadness persisted. She wished that they hadn't come so far away. She longed to be back in New York.

When they got back to the car she took off her wet sneakers and put on dry sandals. Her toes were swollen and waterlogged. Then she took off the watch and cradled it in her palm like a jewel. The rounded, worn case fitted perfectly in her hand. She walked around the car and gave it back to Sam.

"I love it and you're wonderful," she told him. "But I'd rather wait and wear it when we get back to New York." This made her feel better. "As long as we're together I want *you* to be the one who knows what time it is."

"All right," Sam said. He buckled the watch back onto his wrist. Then he looked right at her and smiled. "If you don't want to wear it when we're together," he said, "maybe you'll never get to wear it at all." After that he bent down to unlace his boots and put on his loafers.

She grinned and got back in the car as if nothing had happened. But something had happened and they both knew it. It was the closest either of them had come to mentioning the future—their future. Not too close, but closer. This is it, she thought. This is an important moment. The watch was hers, a promise between them as they drove on north after lunch. For the rest of the afternoon she felt unreasonably happy, just as on the cliffs near Aughris Head she had felt unreasonably sad.

Chapter

4

The road to Sligo lay between high hedgerows which blocked out the view. They got stuck behind messy haywagons and rickety pickup trucks loaded with vegetables in wooden crates. A couple of times Sam had to brake hard to avoid hitting the sheep and goats that straggled into the road through openings in the hedgerows or crowded around the crumbling walls of the narrow stone bridges over brooks and bogs.

Near Strandhill they passed a horse-drawn wooden caravan with a bowed roof like a covered wagon. A string of laundry hung out to dry at the back, and a sleepy-looking male tourist sat in front, watching the fly-studded rump of the plodding draft horse as the hours of his vacation slipped by. *See Ireland by Gypsy Caravan*—she remembered the glossy-looking ads in *The New Yorker*. It didn't look so glossy now; the relentless sound of the horse *clip-clopping* on the pavement, the endless miles of hedgerows blocking out the view, the stuffy interior of the wagon on rainy days. They passed another caravan pulled over to the side of the road. A family of Americans in bright down vests and blue jeans were un-wrapping their musty sandwiches as they sat disconsolate on a dirt bank. An older boy looked up from tethering the horse and gazed longingly at their car.

It was Sunday and for once the streets of the villages were crowded with people. There were children everywhere, every family seemed to have at least four. Red-haired boys with blue eyes teased freckled little girls with dark hair in ragged cotton smocks. Even the vegetables were being wheeled into town for sale in baby carriages and perambulators, whichever conveyance wasn't needed for a child of that age that year. A young boy proudly towed a bright-red wagon filled with the family potatoes.

As they turned north again, the eerie squared-off shape of Ben Bulben loomed ahead of them. *Under bare Ben Bulben's Head / In Drumcliff Churchyard Yeats is laid.* She imagined Yeats's grave among ancient trees in the shadow of this strange green mountain. At Drumcliff the road curved away from Ben Bulben toward the sea. She followed their route on the map as they passed through Grange and Cliffony. Sam stopped for a moment to let a farmer's truck cross in front of them at a flat, empty crossroads. There were no signposts, but on the map the road they were crossing led out to a point of land called Mullaghmore. Where had she heard that name? She groped in her memory for its significance. Then she remembered and fear seeped into her warm good mood like a cold draft. Mullaghmore was where the Provos had killed Mountbatten. She had seen it on television and read about it in *The Times,* and at the time it had seemed so far away. The little fishing boat, lifted out of the water with a great explosion, scattering human bodies over the still surface of the sea. And Mountbatten dead.

The two men who had done it had hidden in these hills and passed this same crossroads in their dilapidated van.

There was a war going on here, with incendiary bombs and snipers and children dying. She and Sam would make a fine target for the I.R.A., she thought, rocketing around in the sports car on these country roads as if they were the Riviera corniches. No, no, they had a reason to murder Mountbatten, although she couldn't remember exactly what it was. They have no reason to hurt us. No reason.

Farther north, the villages they passed seemed darker and grimier. Poor people. The landscape changed again into a bleak, brown wasteland, with jagged peaks of rock pushing up out of the bogs at the side of the road. The hedgerows were gone and she realized how comforting they had been. Sam accelerated on each curve, racing the dying afternoon. The scenery had an ancient, prehistoric look, as if nothing had changed since the time when men lived in caves and hunted with sticks and stones. The light faded and the gray evening threw spooky shadows across their path.

Donegal was an empty town with its center built around a parking lot. On one side of the lot a department store window displayed dusty calico fabrics and broken-looking appliances. On the other side, the shabby facade of the town's principal hotel stood a block above the local chapter of the Sinn Fein—a building plastered with grim posters. The red fist, the silhouette of a man hanging from a gallows, the words written in dripping blood. The hotel's lobby was dark and smelled of damp carpets and boiled cabbage and lonely old men. A surly bellboy led them up to their room with its stained Axminster rugs and chipped Formica furniture. Tattered drapes framed their view of the parking lot and the trampled-down bits of green at its edges.

Instead of having dinner in the dining room, a cavernous salon lined with dusty red-velvet curtains, they walked out into the town, looking for a pub supper. Turning down a narrow street, they found it, a shabby room with an open fire and comfortable chairs, and a friendly publican who was happy to dish them up some stew from the pot his wife had in the kitchen at the back. Hannah rolled the raw warmth of the whiskey in her mouth and let it unknot the worries in her stomach. Sam drank a lot, too. He always did. Not that it ever showed except in his laughing a little more, or seeming more relaxed and affectionate.

She fell asleep quickly, curled numbly against Sam's back between the rough linen sheets. When she woke up again it was still dark. She fought her way up from sleep in a panic. Where was she? Something was going on outside the windows. Looking out, she saw that she had been awakened by raucous serenading coming from a patch of earth around a spindly tree at the south end of the parking lot. A gang of drunken buddies was out there passing the night away, singing and shouting in ragged, unmusical unison. She lay down again and clamped the pillow over her head, but the sound penetrated through the coarse pillowcase and reverberated on the taut strings of her nerves.

"Ohhhh, sheee, married a man with no balls at all . . ." Their voices rose and fell, flatting the high notes and occasionally breaking into bawdy laughter. "No balls at all," they sang, "no balls at all. Ohhhh, sheeeee . . ." Their throats filled the slurred verses with the fervor of drunken camaraderie. She was wide awake now. Sam slept undisturbed beside her, breathing heavily. Lucky Sam. She sat on the edge of the bed. The Irish are great singers, she thought. She remembered the tenor in *The Dead,* and the snow like a cape on the shoulders of Gabriel's overcoat. Singing is general all over Ireland.

She stood up and walked across the room to the bathroom, a tiny cubicle built in sullen obedience to modern tourists' demands for bathrooms. The smell of the drains reminded her of Prince Albert, dying of the typhoid that festered in the royal plumbing at Buckingham Palace. Fear death by drains. Great gurgles and belches grumbled through the bowels of the building, finally exploding into the close air above the sink.

She went back to bed and stared up at the ceiling, trying to block the noise of the singing out of her mind. Maybe this father and son reunion wasn't such a great idea after all. Why hadn't she just stayed out of it? Why did she always have to push everything as far as it would go? Jake and Travis were supposed to meet in Paris and travel to Ireland together. At the time she suggested it, it seemed like the perfect solution. Everything fit. They were about the same age. They were both going abroad alone. And having Jake around would make the meeting of Sam and Travis less difficult. Less intense.

Now this plan seemed fraught with dangers and potential problems. Travis by himself was difficult enough. What if he and Jake hated each other? They probably would. She had hoped that Jake would be friends with Travis and that that would make Travis friendly toward her. What if the opposite happened? Lying there in the dark, she was assailed by fears and doubts. Her head ached, her body felt swollen and grimy. Finally she clamped the pillow back over her ears and fell into a shallow sleep.

She was back in New York. It was springtime, there were tulips in the center strip of Park Avenue and flowers on the bushes in the park. In the dream, she had moved out of her apartment. It had seemed like time for a change. She went back to visit it afterward, to pay a social call on the new tenant. But the apartment looked so wonderful. The bedroom was warm and quiet and light glinted off the carved edges of the big mirror. Sun flooded the living room, and the white linen curtains ruffled gently in the warm spring breeze. She smelled hyacinths and lilacs. And suddenly, with a swift falling in her heart, she realized that this apartment was the only place in the world where she would ever feel safe and whole. Just two rooms. The only possible refuge from the violent world and the harsh, dirty streets outside. She chattered woodenly with the new tenant over a glass of wine, trying not to think—trying not to blurt out her terror. She was disowned and solitary. This apartment was her home, the only home she had, but she didn't live there anymore.

She woke up depressed. The cracked plaster of the ceiling looked dirty, and outside the windows the sky was a dull, unyielding gray. A tiny muscle throbbed in the lid above her left eye. Her stomach felt bloated and sore from the heavy Irish stew they had eaten the night before. Too much Guinness, too much whiskey.

Sam came out of the bathroom and sat on the edge of the bed. His face was pink and healthy from an uninterrupted sleep, and he smelled faintly of cologne. She crunched her grubby body up against the cool, fresh surface of his shirt.

"Dooon't, you're wrinkling it," he said. His cleanliness irritated her. She reached up to muss his carefully combed hair.

"Come on!" He stood up and watched her warily. "What's the matter with you this morning?"

She scrunched down under the covers feeling rejected. "I had a bad dream," she said, pouting. "I dreamed that I had no home."

"Oh, poor sweetie," and he sat down next to her again, putting both arms around her to cuddle and contain her. "Why don't you pack and we'll get going. You'll feel better when we get to Ballymarr and we can settle down for a while."

He was right. She would feel better. Anyway, she hadn't

given up her apartment. It was there, waiting for her, empty, and she could go back to it. The whole thing was just a bad dream. She packed and dressed while Sam went down to the lobby to check out and pay the bill. By the time they left the hotel the sun had burned through the clouds. Donegal looked a lot better on a nice day. They walked down the hill past the Sinn Fein office and along a promenade next to the River Eske. A few swans paddled and dove in the water next to them, veering toward the promenade as if they expected bread. As they watched, more swans sailed toward them from a bend in the river and suddenly there were crowds of swans, drifts of white feathers, lining the banks and croaking hoarsely as they drifted toward the sea.

In the car Hannah's mind drifted comfortingly back to her apartment in New York. Home. Mentally she reached out to caress her books, the comfy old sofa, and the soft blue-and-white rug from a sale at Altman's. New York was wonderful. She had friends there and an okay job and men who were interested enough to take her out for romantic lunches. She was an expert at playing footsie. She thought about Sara and David and the way that Sara kept warning her that she was going to lose David if she kept going out with Sam. She didn't care. She could afford to lose David. He was still there, without her now, working in the office across the hall, walking through the park on his way home after work, sitting at the desk he had built under the loft bed in his little apartment and trying to write a novel in his free time.

Good old David. He had saved her life after her marriage split up; just by being there. Maybe he would find another girl now. Maybe he would keep on hoping. She remembered the pinched, hurt look on his face when she told him she wasn't going to Amagansett, and why.

"Aw, shit, Hannah," he had said, and he turned away from her to look at the bulletin board. There were some postcards and a press release and a few pages of an author's promotional schedule for Philadelphia. He examined them, and then he walked out of the office. She watched his back and thought she probably should have told him about Sam sooner. But since she never believed that Sam was serious, she hadn't wanted to tell anyone about him. Especially not David. She had waited until it was too late, but that was all right. She still half-thought that she would probably end up with David anyway. He was like her—young and struggling and maybe going nowhere—that's why she hadn't wanted to let go of him. She wanted someone to go home to when Sam did the inevitable. Was that so bad?

"He sounds very nice," the psychiatrist said. "Do you think it's fair to go on seeing both of them?"
"Why shouldn't I?"
"The real question is, why should you?"

There were checkpoints along the way as they drove north after Lough Eske and Stranorlar. At the first one, a barrier slowed them down and then a stern-looking Garda officer waved them over to the side. Sam got out of the car and showed him their passports and his driver's license and their international driver's licenses from the AAA, and the car rental and car registration papers. The officer thumbed through them silently and walked around the car.

"Have you had some trouble up here?" Sam said.

The officer didn't answer. He handed Sam back the papers and impatiently waved them on.

At the second checkpoint there were two barriers and a line of policemen, but an officer waved them through without stopping them. As they drove away she noticed a car that had been flagged down for an inspection. It was a gray Morris van with no windows. Its sides were rusted and one fender was dented in against the treadless tires. Two Garda officers were searching it with knives and flashlights, ripping open the dusty padding behind the doors, throwing things from the glove compartment out onto the ground, and examining the greasy undercarriage. Looking for what?

Another man had lifted the hood and was staring in at the engine block. The driver stood silently by. She saw him from behind as they passed, a red-haired kid in black coveralls, standing on one foot as he watched his van get torn apart. She hoped he was innocent and that the police would let him go. Poor guy. But when she looked back at him out the window after they were past, her eyes met his blank, malevolent stare. It looked as if he was memorizing their license number. She hoped they wouldn't let him go.

"I think that guy was memorizing our license number," she said to Sam.

"That's hardly necessary," Sam said. "We're pretty easy to spot."

In every village they drove through now there was a Sinn Fein office. Angry graffiti were splashed on the walls with white paint. *Brits Go Home. Brits Go Home.* Red-and-black posters were pasted up in the towns and on the sides of abandoned farmhouses along the road. The red fist, the silhouette of a man on the gallows, the words written in dripping blood. *Brits go Home. Remember Long kesh. Ireland for the Irish. Support the Hunger Strike.*

"We'll be there by dinner time," Sam said.

Chapter

5

At the end of the afternoon they came to the top of a hill. Ahead they could see the road curving through flat green pastures toward a long glassy lake, with the light as soft as the ringing of silver bells. She took the map out of the glove compartment and refolded it so that the Northern end of Ireland faced up. The lake, Lough Swilly, was at the very end of the island, a sickle-shaped inlet cutting deep into the land from the North Atlantic at Dunaff Head. East of it, on the border to Northern Ireland, Lough Foyle reflected the same long curve like an echo. The map was blotched with green lowlands and brown hills, and the top of Ireland looked ragged and bleak, as if it had been worn away to a skeleton by the sea. She stuffed the map back into the glove compartment.

"Why don't you ever fold it up again?" Sam asked.

"There's no point."

"That ruins the map," he said.

"I don't see how. This way when I want to look at it again it's already folded to the right place."

"Oh."

She opened the compartment and carefully refolded the map, letting it fall into its original accordion so that the top had *Ireland* written on it. And so that the piece she would need to look at was lost again.

In Letterkenny Sam turned up a road marked Rathmullan and after about a mile on that, he turned again down a lane which led in the direction of the water through a thick grove of trees. A copse, she thought. That reminded her of her father's old joke about what Macbeth said when Birnam Wood came to Dunsinane as the prophecy had foretold: "Cheese it, the copse." It still made her giggle inwardly, but she kept it to herself. It wasn't Sam's kind of humor. The lane crossed a narrower track and she noticed a sign: Ballymarr Castle. A castle had been painted, once, in the space below the writing, but now the paint was peeling off and the placard dangled from a post. An arrow pointed to a rutted driveway closed off by two rusted iron gates. Sam got out to open them, and she looked beyond him to what had once been an elegant gatehouse. The Lodge. Now the gothic porticos were chipped and grimy, the heavy wooden front door hung on one hinge below a carved lintel, and torn lace curtains sagged in the windows. The driveway curved uphill beyond it through unclipped rhododendron and laurel hedges that seemed to be taking over the road.

"They were bound to turn the House of Usher into a country hotel sooner or later," she said.

"Let's wait and see before we decide."

They bounced up the bumpy road with pebbles pinging off the bottom of the car and bushes scraping against the side doors. But at the top of the rise, the unruly hedges and brooding oaks opened out onto an immaculate gravel courtyard. Flagstone terraces surrounded an ochre stone castle with turrets and towers so perfectly proportioned that it looked like a toy in spite of its grand size. A Disney Fantasyland castle. Perfect lawns stretched down to a distant river, and crisp white curtains hung in the windows below the parapets. A butler in a black coat stood in the shadow of the great polished mahogany doors.

"May I help you with your bags, sir?" he said.

Another man in livery opened the car door on Hannah's side, and she stepped out onto the gravel like a queen. It made sense to her now. Ballymarr was a secret place, a perfect hideaway, an Irish Meyerling. There wouldn't be many Sunday drivers or casual tourists who would brave the scruffy gates and driveway. It was a remote preserve, isolated even from the rest of Ireland, emptiness within emptiness, poetry within poetry, green within green. The butler led them across the gravel and through the doors into a vast, dark hallway. Oil portraits of racehorses and intricate hunting scenes glimmered in golden frames on the walls. The curves of the great stair, where brass risers held a deep blue Oriental carpet, were punctuated by stained-glass windows and tapestry hangings. The ratty sweater and blue jeans that had been fine for walking around Donegal seemed shabby and out of place.

At the base of the stairs, a row of gleaming bamboo fly rods stood upright in a wooden rack, their long shafts reaching up the stairwell to the second floor. In a side room, tables were being set for dinner with white linen and blue flowers, and at the end of the hall a book-lined library with leather chairs and a marble fireplace commanded a view of the gardens, and the Erninmore River floating in peaceful silver curves toward the lough in the distance.

Upstairs in their bedroom, windows with pale-blue flowered curtains looked out over the same sylvan landscape, and two wing chairs in the flowered pattern flanked the bed.

"This is absolutely heaven," she said, flopping down in

one of the chairs as soon as they were alone together. "Don't you love it? How clever of you to know about a place like this!"

Sam smiled. "I'm very glad you like it," he said. His tone suggested that he had had the entire castle built for her pleasure.

On their way to dinner they explored the other downstairs rooms. Down a long hall in another wing of the castle they found the anglers' bar, a drafty room with a tile floor, where everything revolved around the rough, wet business of fishing. On the wall a detailed map showed the five fishing beats along the Erninmore between the castle and the lough, and underneath it three trout glistened on a slab of marble. Next to it a row of metal hooks on a stand was hung with a pair of waders, a landing net, and a brown tweed jacket out at the elbow. At the wooden bar on one side of the room two gillies, one in a black suit and the other dressed in corduroys and a sweater, turned from their beers to examine Sam and Hannah.

"It's nice to see you here," said corduroy pants in a light brogue, coming over from the bar and reaching out to shake Sam's hand. "I'm Conor Mackin, the head gillie, and I'll be arranging it if you want to do any fishing."

Hannah put out her hand and Conor shook it too. His palm was rough and his fingers were covered with hard, round calluses.

"How's the water?" Sam said.

"Well it's been very low lately, we haven't had as much rain as usual."

"Does that mean we'll be fishing with dry flies?" Sam asked.

"Now, I don't think so, unless you have a desire for that," Conor answered. "They're still taking the Butchers and the Black Gnats all right." The two men fell easily into a discus-

47

sion of flies and water levels and rod lengths. Bloody Butchers, Royal Coachmen and Nymphs. Sam was poised and relaxed as he slipped into the special vernacular of fishing. He was at home anywhere. She felt left out.

It wasn't as if she had never gone fishing, but she could tell right away that fly fishing in Ireland was a very different thing from the trolling she had done with her father, using spinning rods and metal lures. A long time ago. They would get up at dawn and drive north to the lakes, in the old Dodge, through the rosy midwestern beginnings of day. Sometimes she even got to skip school. Memories of those mornings, standing on the wet banks under the dew-dripping trees, stepping into the tippy rowboat he rented, the *whirr* of the reel as the line went out, and the excitement of the first tug and the fish, wriggling and opalescent on the hook.

Jake came with them on those fishing trips sometimes. But he never seemed to care about the fishing, or the rhythms of the lake, or the look of the mist coming off the water. He wasn't exactly a romantic. He was almost ten years younger than she was, but he often seemed much older. Even when he was a child, it was always Jake who got them places on time, Jake who reminded her about doing her household chores, and Jake who arbitrated in family quarrels.

While she and her father went out in the boat, he would settle down precociously with a book and read until they came back. Her father had been disappointed in Jake. He would have liked to school his only son in the manly arts: fishing, sailing, watching sports on television, and drinking beer. But he never got angry about it; Jake seemed to command respect even from his own parents. Her father had settled on her as a surrogate son, and he had taught her everything he knew about the secret currents under the still surface and the flat, mysterious mind of the fish.

"If you're eager for fishing, you could go out tonight," Conor was telling Sam in a low voice. "There's no one on beat two and I saw some fish under the bridge down there earlier in the day."

It was time to get back into the conversation. "Fishing at night?" she said.

"Oh, yes, lady," Conor said. "In the summer it's light enough here until almost midnight. It's a northern place and it's a good time for fishing. The fish cannot see you and they come up to feed."

"Okay," she said. "Let's." She felt suddenly tired again. The long conversation about fishing left her feeling stupid and apprehensive. The bamboo rods in the hall seemed much too long for her to lift. What if she couldn't do it at all? She was hungry. Travis and Jake would hate each other. She was very hungry. It was lunchtime in New York. Why wasn't she there? The beginnings of the long northern twilight gleamed on the river and colored blue and gray the distant foothills of Derryveagh.

In the dining room, a waitress in a black uniform with a tiara of starched white linen led them to a table in the corner.

"I'm starving," Hannah said.

"I'm afraid the food here may not be as good as it should be," Sam said apologetically.

"Almost anything would taste pretty good to me right now."

"Well, we'll see. Irish food is notoriously bad. According to Egon Ronay, the only decent meals to be had are around Galway."

"That *was* good."

"Just don't get your hopes up."

The menu was written out in elegant script on a crackling sheet of parchment. There were no prices, and everything was in French. But the *Soupe Parmentière* was really a lumpy onion-and-potato stew, the *Côtelette de Veau au Duc d'Anjou* was a soggy veal chop that looked as if it had been sitting on a steam table all day, and the *Macédoine de Légumes Provençale* was a heavy silver platter divided into three sections for broiled tomatoes, summer squash, and mushy brussels sprouts. Sam picked at his dinner as if the quality of the food were a personal affront. Hannah eagerly spooned the soup into her mouth.

So it wasn't too tasty; it was food, after all. She loved to eat. Oh, how she loved to eat! She craved the textures of food and its warmth and comforting fillingness—although she was hardly ever too full for just one more bite.

Her mother had tried to keep Hannah from eating by hiding anything fattening. But this just made eating even more fun. There was the search, and then the victory. Delicious. Her happiest memories were of sneaking into the kitchen and uncovering—after an ingenious canvassing of the cupboards—a cache of cookies or chocolate. She knew just how many to take so that it wouldn't be noticeable. She was an expert at eating around the edges of things so that the bites wouldn't show. She was a genius at disguising the spoonprints made in puddings and casseroles by her clandestine raids.

Their table was next to the french doors which led onto the terrace. Below them she could see a series of trellises and gardens going down to the Erninmore. Across the room three men were talking about fly fishing in a conversation which switched back and forth from French to German. At the table next to them an elegant-looking middle-aged couple held hands. They were both wearing wedding rings, but the intensity of their interest in each other's conversation suggested anything but the bored silence and desultory, matter-of-fact dialogues that most married people had in restaurants. The woman was all dressed up in a well-cut mauve-and-pink summer dress which showed off her curvy mature figure. Her heavy blond hair was pulled back from her tanned face in a loose bun. A bottle of champagne with a red stripe diagonally across the label was cooling in a bucket on their table.

"Oh, God, really don't take them to Saint-Tropez," Hannah overheard the woman say in a soft English accent. "We went last year and it was awful. The children were miserable and Allen couldn't find a tennis partner."

"*Now* you tell me," the man said, sounding not at all reproachful. "Fiona's already made reservations. Someone told her there's terrific shopping there. She loves to buy things."

"Crowded boutiques and overpriced pottery," the woman said. The idea of the man having a terrible time seemed to cheer her. He smiled and answered in a lower voice, and Hannah's attention returned to her food.

"Yuck," she said, poking with her dessert fork at the mixture of dried-out cake, watery custard, and ancient strawberries billed as *Gâteau Impériale de Maison,* and trying to find it so unappetizing that she wouldn't go ahead and eat it anyway.

Sam pushed his plate away, his *Gâteau* intact except for one tentative bite. He signaled the waitress for coffee.

She looked around the dining room again, trying to distract herself from the possibility of eating the dessert. The table next to them was empty now, and below her in the garden she saw the middle-aged trysters walking arm in arm through a rose-covered trellis. On the other side of their table was a young, dark-haired couple drinking coffee, and next to them a family of three platinum-blond children and their mother—her hair still a bold blond color but faded by time to mere gold. In the opposite corner, a professorial-looking man sat eating alone with a book propped up against the vase of roses and delphiniums on his table.

By concentrating, she could pick out phrases of French and Italian and German from the general cacophony of dinner-time voices. There were all kinds of people in the room—a roomful of casual tourists—but none of them fit any national stereotype. The Germans weren't gross or blond, the British weren't particularly tweedy, and she and Sam certainly weren't your average camera-toting Americans. Instead, everyone looked rich, with the kind of pleasant, lustrous surface that comes from a life in which almost everything is within reach. The optimism of the privileged.

The rich are their own nation, she thought. Their own nation with their own passports and their own oaths of allegiance and their own ethnic bonds. The waitress came and took away her dessert.

Chapter

6

They stood on the lawn after dinner in the lengthening shadows. Conor prepared the rod and handed it to Hannah, showing her with his wrist and forearm the motion she needed for
a proper cast. Back and then quickly forward. She flubbed it
twice and then she had it. Although the fly was landing on
an Irish lawn instead of the water, the quick movements of
casting began to feel natural to her. The bright fly in the air
above her, the preposterous length and suppleness of the
bamboo rod, the line of white oiled silk across the grass.

"Try to keep the rod between twelve o'clock and two
o'clock." Conor made a wedge in the air with his hands.
"Don't let the rod go back so far."

"Why, Hannah, you're very good at it," Sam said.

Indoors she watched his lithe fingers taking the rod out of
its long soft leather case and choosing a reel from his wooden
reel box with his father's initials on a brass plaque. He
threaded the line through the filigree of metal hoops, holding
it above each hoop to keep it from slipping back down the
rod. After that, he tied a fly onto the invisible leader at the

53

end of the line, using just the tips of his fingers as if he were plucking the strings of some tiny, exquisite musical instrument. The fragile lacquered shafts of wood bent under his touch, acknowledging his mastery.

The Erninmore raced by the rock fishing pier where she stood in the gathering twilight. Upstream, she could see the castle and its quivering mirror image underneath it in the glassy water. The only noise was the distant, raucous gurgle as it broke up and ran over the rapids and the weirs farther down toward the lough. She unhooked the fly from the cork handle of the rod and pulled out a loop of line with her left hand. Step forward, cast back, let the line go tight in the air for a moment, then propel it forward. She jerked the fly along the surface of the water toward her, trying to make it look as if it were alive. Trying to catch the black eye of the trout lurking somewhere below her in the dark water. The fish were canny adversaries hidden in the watery shadows; their undulant silver bodies waved almost imperceptibly as they held their position against the current which drove the river against the pier in a glassy swell.

She felt a tug on the line. Now she could almost sense the fish circling warily up through the levels of darkness toward her. Then there was emptiness again, the fly pulled only by the current, the fish gone. Once she held the rod in the air a beat too long and the fly caught on the gorse bushes at the end of the pier behind her. She put the rod down and followed the line into the prickly underbrush to get it. The stars came out in the pearly sky above the pines.

By the time Sam came to get her, crashing through the brush along the riverbank, it was full dark.

"I've lost the other flashlight, and it's getting late," he said. "Let's quit."

"Okay."

She was surprised that they had been out almost two hours. But when they got back to the castle, and sank into the big chairs in front of the fireplace in the anglers' bar, she was exhausted. Her arm and shoulder ached, and a throbbing blister was forming on the soft inside of her index finger. Only two fish had been caught, both by the youngest man at the table of three she had noticed at dinner. He was preening at the bar, speaking in proud German gutturals to one of his dining-room buddies. The fish lay luminescent on the slab.

"I think Travis will really like it here," Sam said. "He always loved fishing."

"When do you expect him?" Hannah asked. Her voice sounded shrill. "What's the plan?"

"He was originally supposed to meet Jake in Paris sometime last week and then come up here with him," Sam said. "There was a message from him when we got here, though, saying that he was on his way from Dublin. I guess Jake will come a little later. What's this, Monday? Travis ought to be here in a day or two. Hello, it's nice to meet you, congratulations on your catch." Conor had brought the young German over to where they were sitting and they all shook hands.

"Thank you very much," he said. His English was perfect; he was attractive but very young. About her age. He took a flat metal box out of his side pocket and popped it open to show Sam and Conor. Inside were neatly arranged rows of flies that he had tied himself for the fishing at Ballymarr. Black and red and blue with pieces of yellow, and brown with pieces of white and green, and green with a spot of red feather. He took out three little black ones with a tuft of yellow and handed them to Sam.

"Here, try these tomorrow," he said.

Clip, clip, clip. Five splashes. *Slap, slap, slap.* The sounds of the morning came through the door from the bathroom across the hall. Her arm ached, her back was stiff, her blister smarted and stung. She peered out warily from her warm refuge between the soft sheet and the feather pillows.

Sam bounced into the room all ready to go. His skin gleamed from warm water and shaving lotion, and he was wearing a green angler's tackle jacket and deeper-green corduroys. He hummed Vivaldi to himself as he tucked an assortment of flies and equipment into his pockets.

"Couldn't I just lie here and recover this morning?" she said, her body dragging as she pulled herself out of the covers and up to a sitting position. "Ouch. I think the jet lag has caught up with me."

"Oh, come on, you're just having a first-timer's aches and pains. You'll feel fine when we get out there—*if* we ever get out there."

Sam was right, of course. By the time she was up and walking behind Conor down the river bank in the fragrant morning, she was glad she hadn't stayed in bed. He led them to a grassy spot under a stone bridge, and she could see flashes of the trout clustering on the other side of the river. In midstream, others held their shimmering bodies almost still against the sandy bottom. One jumped above the surface, making a perfect blue-and-gray arc above the water.

"Looks like a fine day for us," Conor said. Then he cast. The fly soared back behind him in slow motion and looped forward, lighting weightlessly on the water's skin just over the group of feeding fish near the opposite bank. One trout separated itself from the nacreous mass and followed the fly for a moment, its body waving softly on the other side of the mirror of the surface. There was a jerk against the rod, and Conor quickly put it down and played the fish in with his hands on the line, finally flipping it up onto the grassy shore with a quick movement of his wrists.

Standing above one of the deep pools on the other side of the bridge, she tried to imitate Conor's magic. She cast out, and the line went straight toward the edge of the pool. An indistinct shape left the shadows and swam toward the fly, hesitating about four feet away. She cast again, arm back and then forward. Poetry in motion. The fly landed softly just above the fish. The rod bobbed, she felt a sudden pull, and her heart leaped. She pulled against the line to set the hook, and the rod bent dangerously down toward the water. The white silk ratcheted out of the reel with a long shriek.

"Hey, I got one!" she shouted, trying to slow the race of the line without putting too much pressure on it. Conor hurried over. The trout thrashed in the pool and then disappeared into the depths. She let him have the line, leaving it slack enough to keep it from breaking under the strain, playing the fish at the fine edge of its endurance.

The rod jerked back and forth and her heart pounded against the front of her chest. I want him, she thought. I want this big trout. Slowly she reeled the line in, balancing its flexibility against the fading strength of the fish. Abruptly the rod stopped its crazy whipping motions and she felt a heavy weight at the end of the line. She flipped her wrist up and dropped the fish into the landing net that Conor held out for her.

"Good work," he said.

The big trout lay on the grass. His body flapped against the ground and the morning sun picked out each translucent scale and belly spot. Conor yanked the hook out of his bony mouth and quickly broke his back against the rocks. The canny adversary lay suddenly still, color and life ebbing out of him as she watched. A dead fish. Hannah felt excited and sad. She wished that the trout had fought harder. Now that it was over, she wished he had won.

Chapter

7

She glared unhappily at her image in the full-length mirror on the back of the bedroom door. The gabardine skirt was wrinkled and the blue sweater made her look lumpy. She pulled up the waistband of the sweater and bloused it out around her hips. No improvement. Sam opened the door from the other side and her image vanished.

"Are you ready yet, sweetie?" he said. He looked wonderful, very elegant but just casual enough for a dinner party at a neighboring Irish castle.

"Not quite," she said. She peeled off the blue sweater and took her beige silk shirt out of the drawer. The waistband of the skirt was crumpled and tight, but maybe with a belt it would be all right. She put on the shirt and buckled the narrow leather belt, closing the door to look at herself in the mirror again. Her hips looked big and the shirt was a little too formal. She wanted to make a good impression on these friends of friends of Sam's who had invited them to a dinner party at Castle Tyrone, on the other side of the lough. She was nervous, and she noticed sweat stains under the arms of the shirt as she tried to adjust her clothes.

"You look fine, sweetie," Sam said. "That looks very

nice." The idea of going to a stranger's dinner party in a foreign country didn't seem to bother him in the least.

She took off the belt and silk shirt and tried another sweater. An old yellow one with a nice scoop neck. It looked good against the khaki skirt, but the color made her face seem mousy and washed out. Dark colors were better on her. If only she had brought her blue blazer, it would have been perfect over the skirt and sweater.

"Come on, kiddo, we're going to be late," Sam said. "Really, that looks fine." He was beginning to sound impatient. She took off the yellow sweater and put the blue one back on. At least it was the right color.

"Okay, let's go," she said, giving her hair a last, nervous comb. She didn't look right, but there was nothing to be done about it. She felt uncomfortable and anxious and fat. And Sam's friend of a friend, Frederick Culloden, sounded like just the kind of man who would notice. Sam had called him yesterday, and he insisted that they come for dinner. He had dinner parties every night. She imagined the upper-class voice honking her death knell: What a lovely girl, now *where* did you say she went to school? She wondered how much Sam would be influenced by Culloden's perception of her, and she worried.

On the drive over, Sam told her everything he knew about Culloden. He was a man who collected beautiful things: paintings and racehorses and antique cars. After the war he had come to Ireland and bought the wreck of Castle Tyrone for almost nothing. He rebuilt the historic walls and planted vast gardens, stocked the streams with salmon and decorated the interior with paintings and tapestries and period furniture. Tyrone was his home, although, Sam speculated, he probably spent a lot less time there than he spent visiting with friends on the Ile Saint-Louis or in the Sussex countryside or at Porto Ercole and Cap d'Antibes.

59

Mediterranean villages, summer places, ski houses at Sugarbush and islands in Maine. White is for brides and linens; black is for caviar and funerals—and a few old servants who have been with the family for years. This was Sam's world. She felt more and more out of place as the car wound up a hill through two sets of white-painted cast-iron gates and down through a maze of elaborate topiary hedges to a massive gray stone porte cochere.

A man in a tweed cap and plus fours came out to hold the car doors for them and then drove it away to some invisible garage. Another man, in green-and-gold livery, led them to an upstairs sitting room. Flanked by four greyhounds at rest, Culloden stood there in front of a fire set on gleaming brass andirons under a lavender marble mantelpiece. He was a tall, heavy-set man with baby-soft white hair, big brown eyes, and smooth pink cheeks. It was hard to imagine him doing anything more strenuous than greeting dinner guests. Hannah held his cool, plump hand for a moment, and then he leaned over to take Sam's hand and kiss the air on each side of his face.

"Dear boy," he said. "I feel as if I know you well. How wonderful that you could come, I'd like you to meet Conte Alessandro Vincetti." Then he drew Sam away toward a slim young man who wore a pale-yellow cashmere sweater, and Hannah was left to fend for herself.

Against the bookshelves on the other side of the room, a blonde woman with an expensively weathered face was chatting with a plump, creamy-looking woman in a low-cut beige chiffon evening dress. (The blue sweater was definitely too informal—she should have worn the silk shirt.) Near them, a red-faced man in a velvet jacket looked silently out the window at the gardens.

"It's a lovely view," Hannah said, joining him by the window.

"Oh, yes, certainly, a lovely view," he said, clearing his

throat. He was wearing velvet slippers embroidered with foxes' heads.

"Do you live near here?" she asked, leaning toward him in an effort to capture his attention. He continued to gaze vaguely out the window.

"Yes, yes, we do live near here," he said. "That's my wife." As he waved to the woman in the beige chiffon his face was animated for a moment by a possessive smile, then his features lapsed back into beefy immobility.

Hannah moved toward the two women; the blonde one was talking to the beige chiffon in a dramatic, whispery voice.

"My *dear*," she hissed, "she was just standing there without a *stitch* on! Tony said he had *never* been so embarrassed in his whole *life*."

"How *awful*," the other woman said in a louder voice, but with the same emphatic accent.

"Thank *God* the General was there," the blonde woman went on. "He wrapped her right up in the piano shawl and led her away."

Hannah wandered back toward Culloden, stopping to admire an important arrangement of gladiolas, tuberoses, and snapdragons from the garden, and taking a miniature quiche lorraine off a silver tray on the center table.

"And how is dear Angelica?" Culloden was saying to Sam as she approached. "I'm *so* delighted that she persuaded you to call me."

Alessandro turned to Hannah. She had just popped the little quiche into her mouth, leaving an explosion of crumbs on the front of her blue sweater.

"Do you know la Bella Angelica?" he asked. "Are you one of Angelica's friends?"

She chewed frantically to free her mouth for an answer. Alessandro's gaze flicked away from her to the other guests.

"No," she said finally, "I'm a friend of Sam's."

"Ohhhh," Alessandro brought his attention back to her with wide-eyed mocking surprise. "A friend of Sam's but not a friend of Angelica's? But she is so lovely, *incantevole,* so charming."

"How nice," Hannah said. At her feet, on a pale-green Aubusson, one of Culloden's greyhounds yipped and quivered in its sleep, its bony gray body vibrating with bad dreams. She bent down to stroke the short fur on its gaunt muzzle. The dog woke up and growled angrily at her.

"Diana!" Culloden said. "Mind your manners."

The butler appeared in the doorway, and Culloden started out of the room, leaning on Alessandro's arm. Sam politely offered his arm to the beige chiffon; the blonde woman and the velvet jacket fell into step; and Hannah walked uncomfortably at the end of the line. In the dim light of the hall she quickly brushed the crumbs off her sweater, pulling the fabric out to dislodge them. She looked up and saw that she was being watched by another butler, who stood in a doorway to one side of the stairs. His face was absolutely still, his eyes expressionless.

She felt a little better when they got to the dining room and she saw that her place card was propped in a silver bracket on Culloden's right. The blonde woman gave her a jealous look. The table was set with oversized silver flatware with gold handles, and another gigantic flower arrangement dominated the center space, separating her from Sam, who was leaning solicitously over the beige chiffon's considerable décolletage.

When a pale pink soup was served in Beleek soup dishes with twisted handles, Culloden took a pill from each of three silver boxes in front of him on the table, and swallowed them with a glass of water poured from a silver pitcher at his place.

"You can't be too careful with your health," he said, turning to confide in her as he dipped his spoon into the soup.

"It's a lovely soup," she said, trying to sound as if she knew something about soup.

"Oh, yes, Michel is quite wonderful. I hired him away from the Duchesse de la Selle last year. She wasn't very gracious about it, I must say." He laughed, looking right into Hannah's eyes and inviting her to laugh with him. For the first time all evening she felt engaged in a conversation. She began to relax.

"Now, let's see, you live in New York, is that right?" he asked.

"Yes, we've only been in Ireland a few days."

"Did you get to Paris on your way here?"

"No—well, Sam did, but I came straight to Shannon from New York."

"Oh, dear girl, you must get him to take you back to Paris. You have to see the new Beaubourg museum," Culloden said. "I know you would like it. Of course, it's been terribly controversial, but it's a dazzling building if you ask me." He spoke as if quite a few people had asked him.

"I'd love to see it," she said. The conversation faltered. Her soup spoon clinked against the delicate plate. Were you supposed to tip the bowl away from you or toward you to spoon out the last of the soup? Culloden picked his up by the handles and drank it off.

"This is a wonderful castle," she said. "You must love living here."

"Oh, yes, I've been able to do great things with this place. They've made it a National Monument, and of course that's quite a compliment to me. It was the castle of great Irish chieftains years ago, the Earls of Tyrone, and I like to think those old fellows would approve. Did you know that when O'Neill fled, the legend has it that he left for Rathmullan from here? Fascinating, don't you think?"

"Oh, really?" Of course, she didn't know what he was

talking about. But at that moment, just as she was about to ask, the soup plates were cleared. Culloden gave her one last twinkling smile and turned his complete attention to the blonde woman, seated on his left. Hannah was left to talk with the red-faced man in the velvet slippers, who had—as had everyone at that precise moment—stopped conversation with the guest on one side and turned to the guest on the other side.

"I was glad that you got to talk to Frederick at dinner," Sam said as they drove out of the gates at last. "Did you have a nice time?"

"It's a fabulous place," she said. "He was starting to give me a terrific Irish history lesson. Did you hear him talking about the history of the castle?" She was certainly not going to mention Angelica, or Alessandro's gibes, or the poker-faced butler in the hallway. She knew that Sam knew she had been uncomfortable, but she wasn't going to give him the satisfaction of complaining about it. If she did, he would just apologize anyway, in a tone of voice that would make her feel clumsy and put down.

"I'm so sorry, sweetie," he would say. "We won't go there again if you didn't enjoy it."

But she wasn't going to give him the chance. He could stuff Angelica and the rest of his gorgeous rich friends for all she cared. Bunch of faggots. She wasn't like that, she was magnificent.

"I guess I didn't hear him talking about history," Sam said. "He's a fascinating man, though. Wasn't the lamb delicious?"

Chapter

8

She found the Encyclopedia in the bookshelves of the library before breakfast. Putting her cup of coffee on one of the round tables in front of the fireplace, she reached up and took down the I–J volume. Plumes of dust came off the pages of the musty old book, and she wiped the dark-blue cover with the sleeve of her sweater before resting it on the writing table.

The thin paper crackled as she turned to the history of Ireland. Under Ulster, she read about Queen Maeve and the Ulster Cycle and Cuchulain battling the waves. She turned the page to the story of the O'Neills and the Red Hand of Ulster. O'Neill had sailed against the rival chieftains in a race to Ulster—the first one who landed would claim it. He won by hacking off his right hand and throwing it ashore.

She turned the page again. Skipping the Vikings and John de Courcy, she finally found Hugh O'Neill, the Earl of Tyrone. O'Neill had led a series of heroic rebellions against the British in the sixteenth century.

"Although the chieftains had little military success," she

read, "their bristling presence prevented the British Crown from taking over the lands of Ulster outright. Although he held the British title of Earl of Tyrone, O'Neill was continually harassed by sheriffs and officers of the King. The English government suspected him of plotting another insurrection, and his followers were warned that the King's men were preparing to arrest him."

This information may have been false, but O'Neill was an old man and the last of the great chieftains. O'Donnell had already fled to Spain, Maguire had been killed in the last uprising, and O'Cahan had died in the Tower of London after his capture. A clansman procured a ship for O'Neill's escape and he boarded it at Rathmullan on Lough Swilly. O'Donnell's son Rory, the Earl of Tyrconnell, and one hundred of Ulster's leaders, priests, and chieftains, went with them. O'Neill's son Con, who was living in hiding, was also to have gone, but he apparently did not receive the message, and he did not appear at the docks. O'Neill wanted to wait for his son, but over his protests the ship finally set sail for France at midnight, carrying the last hopes of a Gaelic Ireland with it.

"The Flight of the Earls," as this exodus is called, left Ireland leaderless and virtually helpless against the British. The Catholic lands of Ulster were forfeited by the Crown, and the Irish were resettled on the area's most infertile land. The good land was repopulated by immigrant Scottish and English Protestants, and the city of Derry was given to the citizens of London.

"This Night Sees Ireland Desolate," by Aindrais Mac-Marcuis, is one of many dirges written about the Flight of the Earls.

"Men smile at childhood's play no more
Music and song their day is O'er. . . ."

66

Her eye skipped down the page to the last stanza.

"Her Chiefs are gone. There's none to bear
Her cross or lift her from despair;
The grieving lords take ship. With these
Our very souls pass overseas."

She closed the heavy blue volume and looked out at the gardens. The water of the Erninmore in the morning light curved gently down toward Lough Swilly, where the long docks at Rathmullan were just hidden behind the hills after the next curve of the shoreline.

She imagined an old man pacing in Culloden's parlor, staring out at the moorlands, making his decision. A coat upon a stick, once proud, now walking with the halt steps of the aged. Down to the docks. Servants with trunks and bundles. A great sailing ship with masts rigged and mizzens set. A procession of loss.

Sam startled her out of her daydream with an imperceptible sound. He was standing in the doorway, and his face, thrown into relief by the morning light, looked twisted and anxious. His lips were tightly pressed together and his jaw clenched.

"Come on, let's have breakfast," he said. "I just got a message from the people Travis stayed with in Donegal last night. He's coming into the Letterkenny bus station on a Donegal coach that gets in this afternoon. We'll drive down to meet him and pick him up, okay?"

Chapter

9

It took Travis more than two hours to get a message through by telephone to Ballymarr Castle from the General Post Office exchange in Dublin. He stood in a phone booth on one side of a high-ceilinged room with pale-green linoleum floors. First the lines were out of order, then the lines were busy. He didn't mind. He didn't really have anything else to do, and from the glass window of his booth he could watch the operator behind a desk at the other side of the room as she tried to put through his calls.

"Are you married?" he teased her in a half-joking, half-flirting way. "I bet you have a lot of guys who want to marry you." She was pretty enough, and it was fun to see her respond to him through the glass, blushing and giggling and pretending not to look up at him.

She studied him from under her lashes when she hoped he wasn't looking. A lanky American with floppy brown hair and long legs in faded jeans. Maybe he was one of those rich boys you read about in the dailies, hitchhiking around Europe for the experience before they take over the family bank or something. Maybe he would fall in love with her and take her back home to America with him. Maybe she would have a grand life and a big house with pictures on the walls and real velvet chairs. Maybe she would never have to go back to the dingy little flat off Merrion Street and her bitch of a mother again.

"I'll meet you after work if you like," she said. He loped out of the building without a glance backward when his call had gone through, and she wondered if he really would come back to see her when her shift was up. Probably not. But at six o'clock there he was, standing at the bottom of the steps to O'Connell Street.

They walked down toward the Liffey together, and later she took him to a cafe behind the Abbey Theatre where you could get a Guinness and a sandwich for not too dear, and you could sometimes catch a glimpse of a famous actor—someone like Siobhan McKenna or Brian Farley.

Travis told her about his trip north from Paris. The train and the boat and the train and the boat. He chattered about Paris and the Louvre and the way everything looked like an old postcard. She had never been to Paris, but she had been to London once. They talked about England and he told her about the friends he had made on the long ride up to Liverpool and what a great bargain the Eurailpass was for Americans. He described the trip across the Irish Sea and coming into Dublin at dawn. After dinner he offered to walk her home, but she didn't want him to. She didn't want him to see how she lived, and anyway, her Mum would make trouble.

"I'd come with you instead, if you wanted that," she said, and she smiled nervously down at the sidewalk. Dimples, dark hair, the plump curve of her cheek.

"No, thanks, maybe I'll call you again when I'm back in Dublin." And he shook her hand and swung off down the street, taking her dreams with him.

Well, he just wasn't up for it that night. Not with all the complications and starting north again tomorrow. She was too eager anyway. There had been times during dinner when he wanted her, all right, but at the end there was a tiny edge of desperation in her voice that turned him off. He wanted it, he always wanted it, and he hadn't fucked anyone since that skinny girl on the night train outside of London. But this girl was a little too willing.

He liked it better if there was some game to it, some resistance before they let you do it, so that in the end you felt like you had won something. He loved it when they pretended that they didn't want it at all, fighting hard in his arms when they knew damn well it was too late.

He walked back to the bed-and-breakfast on Rutland Street and went up the narrow stairs to his room. He had paid five pounds in advance, handing the money to an old hag in a dirty flowered dress, who had pointed out his doorway. He switched on the light and stood by the window. Grime and city soot splattered in abstract patterns against the glass. Now that he had turned the girl down he was excited. He stood by the bed and closed his hands around his cock and thought about her, about pulling up her skirt over her plump white thighs and pushing and sucking her nipples and forcing her legs apart. His hand moved quickly up and down, and now he was up inside her, hot and pushing deeper while she still fought him, her body caught on his cock, his whole body releasing, and that wonderful feeling.

He took off the rest of his clothes and brushed his teeth in the basin at the corner of the room. A brown stain spread across the white porcelain bowl away from the drain; the water came out in stingy drips. He turned the switch for the fly-specked bare bulb that hung from the ceiling and crawled in between the heavy, damp sheets.

Morning was clear and warm, a few rays of sunshine filtered in through the dirty window. Travis shaved and sponged himself off with cold water from the tap. He stuffed his washcloth and toothbrush into the side compartment of his green backpack, put the toy monkey Callie had given him in the top so that the little fellow could look out without being seen, and walked the ten blocks to the Amiens Street station.

On the train to Donegal he sat next to a fat, red-haired schoolteacher with freckles on every inch of his skin. The schoolteacher told Travis that he was taking a vacation from his job in Dublin to visit his married sister in the North. Her husband had a bad back and he'd be in bed for a while. Travis told the teacher about his trip north from Paris. The long train rides, the great deal he got by buying his Eurailpass in New York, the dawn over Dublin.

"What takes you to Donegal?" the man asked. Travis explained that he was going to meet his father.

"I haven't seen him in two years," he said. "I hope he'll be glad to see me." He tried to laugh.

The fat man nodded sympathetically as if with some inner knowledge and wisdom. A freckled Buddha. He reached into his battered black briefcase for a cracked leather flask of whiskey and passed it to Travis.

"There now, lad, have some," he said. "Will you be doing any fishing up north?" Travis took a pull from the flask, trying to taste and swallow as little as possible without being rude.

"I hope to," he said. But when the train pulled into Donegal Station his new friend was swept off by a large family of children and chattering women in black dresses, and he was left alone on the deserted platform.

It was late afternoon and he wandered down the street toward the village green, a rim of grass and trees around a parking lot. He walked under the trees toward the stone facade of the hotel which faced the parked cars; pretty shabby, but it was too expensive for him anyway. An empty Paddy's bottle lay against the roots of a big chestnut tree. It was half filled with rainwater and looked as if it had been there for days. Travis had nowhere to stay, he had nowhere. Why hadn't that stupid fat schoolteacher invited him home?

Leaning forward and readjusting his pack, he headed down a side street toward the river. Bed-and-breakfast time, another hag with an angry face and torn stockings, another lonely night of beating off in a lonely cubicle and sleeping on a hard single bed. That could wait. He stopped in a small, dark pub on a side street to soften his growing sense of isolation with a few beers. Donal O'Grady, the publican, noticed him when he ordered his third. A clean-cut American kid with a friendly face and big brown eyes. Maybe that was the way his nephews in Boston looked now—except for Mikey's bright red hair. He hadn't seen the boys since his brother decided to look for work in America, to join their cousin in Massachusetts. Their letters made it sound like the promised land, but Donal figured a lot of that was just the same old-world blarney. He let the rules slip a bit this gray afternoon and poured himself a little whiskey.

"Traveling?" he asked the kid as he put the heavy beer mug down on the bar.

"Yes, sir, I am," said Travis.

In the end, he spent the night in a narrow bunk above ten-year-old Gerald O'Grady's bed in the publican's quarters above the pub. Mrs. O'Grady was a plump, worn-out-looking woman with a big laugh. Her homemade dinner of boiled potatoes and cabbage and lamb stew tasted delicious after days of soggy sandwiches and cafeteria hot plates.

"This is a lovely dinner, ma'am," Travis said. The two O'Grady children jostled and teased each other at the table and made curious eyes at their American guest.

Later, in front of the fire after closing hours, the two men drank the rest of the bottle of whiskey. Travis hated hard liquor, but there was no way out of it. He drank as little as he could, and Donal got drunk. First he told Travis about his nephews in Boston and extracted a promise that Travis would look them up if he was ever there. Then he started in about Ireland. His eyes glazed over with liquor and sentiment as he recited the stories of Irish myth and history. The peat fire gave off a pleasant smell and the warmth and the whiskey made Travis drowsy. Donal droned on through Queen Maeve and the Spanish invasion and O'Neill's great defeats. The litany of losses went on and on; Travis began to have trouble staying awake.

He had never been any good at history. Dates seemed to juggle themselves around or reverse their numbers in his mind. He always got things backward or in the wrong order —when he got them at all. There must have been a time when he knew as much as the other kids in his class, but he couldn't remember such a time. All he could remember was being behind and not understanding and the gut-wrenching humiliation of being called on in class. He would stand there stammering and blushing and wish he was dead. The girls giggled at him—although he usually made them sorry afterward, one way or another.

Brigid O'Grady was about that age. He wondered what she'd look like in a few years. Lolita. Already she was a cute little number with her mischievous, inquisitive blue eyes, and her beginning titties pushing out through her sweater. He had something to show her all right. He thought about her body as Donal chanted on through the Flight of the Earls, the Fall of Parnell, and the Easter Uprising. Finally his long sad story was over and he slumped down in his chair in front of the last coals of the fire. The bottle of whiskey was empty. Donal seemed to have forgotten that Travis was there at all. Supporting himself against the chair and the door frame, he shuffled out of the room. Travis heard him thump up the narrow staircase and creak across the floorboards down the hall. Then there was the high squeaking of bed-springs and silence.

Staring at the dying fire, he was swamped by a great wave of loneliness. Everything was so sad. Everything was so complicated and full of pain. His own eyes teared up as he thought about his life and its pointlessness. Sure, people had loved him along the way, but what good was that? He was an overgrown highschool dropout on his way to beg favors from his famous father. He loved his father, but he hated his father. Images from the past flashed through his mind: his father's coldness, his father's suave disdain, his father's way of making Travis feel that he was from some kind of vaguely inferior species.

He was flattered to be invited to Ireland. Then, after he had said yes, they had paired him up with that creep Jake Bart. Jake was the kind of college smartass who made Travis glad he hadn't gone on in school. Jake could always think of a dozen uptight reasons not to do something. Jake was always spouting quotes from books. Jake was always just mentioning his successes at Harvard. Why should he have to put up with the prudish kid brother of his father's current girl friend? Why couldn't his father have made it just a reunion between the two of them? Father and son. He remembered the story of the Prodigal Son from Sunday School, and resentment simmered in his drunken heart.

After a while he climbed the narrow stairs to Gerald's room and his bunk for the night. If only it were Brigid in the lower bunk instead of her brother. She would be waiting up for him, covered to the chin but with those sparkling eyes just asking for it. As he looked down at the child's sleeping form, Gerald cried out.

"Daddy, Dad"—a mumbled plea from some dark place on

74

the other side of sleep. In the dim light from the hall, Travis saw his swollen sleeper's face rolling on the pillow and the sweaty peaks of his tousled red hair. "Dad, Daddy." Poor kid. Travis sat down on the edge of the bed and held Gerald's shoulders for a moment, sheltering the boy's body from the darkness with his own.

"That's all right," he said softly. "That's all right, it's going to be all right." Gerald settled back into sleep with a long sigh, and Travis quietly climbed up the headboards to the empty bunk.

10

Fenders scraped against tires and the old red-and-white coach belched exhaust fumes as it chugged out the Donegal Road toward Letterkenny. Travis shut his window against the smell. It looked as if the Irish hadn't heard about emission control yet, but there were so few cars on the road that it probably didn't matter anyway. Ireland was the emptiest place he had ever seen. It made him feel lonely. The bus rattled for miles over rocky moors and through peat bogs. An old farmer in heavy boots warmed a teakettle over a peat fire at the edge of a field, but otherwise there were no signs of people except the roofless ruins of a few stone cottages. Where had they all gone?

Sheep and goats scrambled out of the road away from the passing bus. Inside, it smelled of stale beer and cigarette smoke, and the man sitting next to him picked at a soft pack of Players with a horny yellow fingernail. The man was pasty-looking, with greasy black hair. He was wearing a shiny dark-blue suit with a ragged crew-neck sweater underneath it and no shirt, and when he smiled his teeth were yellow, too.

"Would you like a smoke, lad?"

Travis declined and looked determinedly out the window at the abandoned landscape. He didn't exactly feel like getting picked up by a dirty old man on this dirty old bus. He imagined his father's reaction if he got off at Letterkenny with a grimy Irish companion. Anyway, he hated smoking. It was a disgusting habit. Dirty and messy and really insane if you looked at the pictures of what it did to your lungs. That was one of the things that had always bothered him about his father. He took such good care of himself but in Travis's opinion he blew the whole thing when he lit up a cigarette in that ridiculous affected way he had. His stomach turned over nervously, they were almost there. He hugged the top of the backpack and scratched the little monkey between his cloth ears. Callie had cried when she gave it to him.

"I just know if you go and see your father you won't come back here," she had said.

"Don't be dumb, Callie, of course I'll come back," he'd said. But he knew that she was right. His life would never be the same after this trip. His dad wanted to see him, and he could change everything. No more working on a sheep ranch and making promises to the owner's daughter and doing odd jobs for three dollars an hour. No way. Maybe he could even get his diploma now and go into publishing too. He was open to that; after all, it was the family business. He'd have to start from the bottom, of course, but he didn't mind. He wouldn't get a swelled head about it like some of the guys from school he had talked to who were already in law school or pre-med or jobs in journalism and thought they were better than everyone else.

No, he would be the kind of editor people talked about in important places. An editor who really understood the problems writers had and knew how to help them. After all, he had been out there in the cold himself and he knew what it was like.

"Why don't you ask Travis Noble to read your manuscript?" people would say. "He has an open mind."

The bus swayed through miles of fields, with brown cubes of peat stacked up by the side of the road like flat building blocks. In the distance, a bent figure hacked at the hard soil with a primitive wood-and-iron tool. Well, if he went into publishing his father would be proud of him, anyway, and that would be a welcome change. Maybe all the teachers who had given up on him would wish they hadn't, too. Maybe even the headmasters would be a little sorry. Eat your heart out, Dr. Sloane! he thought with a grin as the bus rounded a bleak corner in the road.

"I'm disappointed in you, Travis." That's what they had all said with this grim look on their pruny old faces. They wore horn-rimmed glasses, tweed jackets, and flat brown shoes with laces. Dr. Sloane had said it as they walked across the lower school playing field in the New Hampshire spring mud. It oozed up over Travis's worn sneakers, but Sloanie's cordovans stayed miraculously clean and shiny.

Dr. Peabody had said it as Travis sat uncomfortably on the couch in the paneled headmaster's study at Southfield, rain splatting against the stained-glass windows. Even Mr. Mayer had said the same thing, mumbling into the piles of papers on his desk the day he called Travis into his windowless office at Bristol Academy for the last time. Shit. He wasn't going back to another place like that, anyway. Going off to some snobby boarding school was never his idea. He hated them. Nobody even noticed how many friends he had or mentioned that he was nominated for the student council or that he saved the track season. They cheered hard enough when he was out there running and winning for them. Old Coach Edwards was the only teacher at Bristol who even bothered to say goodbye.

78

It wasn't like that out west. Out there no one cared where you went to school or what you were planning to major in or who your father was. He had worked hard and supported himself and people liked him. It was more than two years since anyone had said he was disappointed in Travis and that was fine with him. In fact, he had half-decided never to go back east at all before he heard from his dad. After that, everything he had been so satisfied with began to seem a little boring. Why should he waste his life on a sheep ranch when great opportunities were waiting for him? New York, Paris, Dublin. Just saying those names out loud made him see what a dumpy little one-horse town he had almost been preparing to settle down in. He started packing.

Of course, he wasn't exactly thrilled when he got his ticket and the letter about meeting Jake in Paris. It almost sounded as if his father didn't trust him on his own. He had at least tried to get some idea of what the girl was like from Jake, but Jake was too uptight to talk about girls. During the week they spent together at the youth hostel in Neuilly Jake had never gotten angry, or drunk, or horny—even though Helen, one of the girls at the hostel, had a terrific crush on him. What a dog. He hated it when she and Jake and the other Harvards he knew got together and talked about stuff he couldn't understand. The best thing he did was get out of there and head north early; Jake was supposed to follow him in a few days. Travis hoped he wouldn't bother.

At least the girl didn't sound like another one of his father's glamourpusses. They all looked the same—bony, with no tits and too much makeup—and they all treated him like a kid. This girl at least had a real-sounding name. Hannah. Not Angelica, my dear, or Bianca, or Pippa short for Philipa. It was a pretty funny name, though. Hannah Banana, that's what they called the nurse's daughter at Bristol Academy. If this Hannah had tits like that Hannah, at least he'd have something to look at. That Hannah was fat, but she put out. The guys were always teasing her because she was the nurse's daughter and she liked it so much. "Ohhhhh," they'd say, "I have this terrible pain between my legs, please help me, nurse," and stuff like that. Pretty tasteless.

One day he walked Hannah Banana behind the chapel after dinner and kissed her and copped a big feel, slipping his hands under her sweater and her stiff cotton bra and rubbing her nipples while he pressed up against her. He heard she was one of the girls who sometimes went with a few guys up to the abandoned shed behind the football field. There were girls from town who would do anything. The guys would chip in some money and get a girl who would come and take off all her clothes and they could all touch her anywhere as much as they wanted to. Sometimes they fucked too.

He had been invited to chip in and go along once, but he wasn't about to get involved in anything like that. The next thing you knew, the girl's father was having a serious conference with the headmaster and the girl was pregnant and they all tried to make you feel ashamed you had fucked her and lucky about having to marry her. That happened to a kid named Kimmy Hunt the year he was at Southfield. They had the wedding at the Episcopalian Church in town and a lot of people from the school were invited. The girl was hanging on to Kimmy's arm like she had won him at a raffle or something. Kimmy and his parents looked like they had just swallowed a great big mouthful of rocks and were having trouble smiling and getting them down at the same time.

The bus jounced through the outskirts of Letterkenny. Out the window he saw stone houses with blue and green curtains instead of doors and a garage where an old Austin Princess was jacked up on a rack. A mechanic was standing underneath the car, gazing vaguely up at the gearbox and holding a bottle of Guinness. He was almost there.

Even seeing his mom had been easy compared to this. He

had stopped off at the house in Ashmont and they had actually had a nice time together. She was a lot better with his father gone for good. It used to be so bad. Some childhood. She would sit at the kitchen table with her sherry instead of lunch and read all the movie magazines and the *National Enquirer* and all that crap, and sometimes she would find a story about Sam and some other woman or Sam and his glamorous single life and she'd burst into tears.

When he got home from school she'd be hunched over the table, a filter-tip cigarette smoldering in the tin ashtray and the bottle of sherry half empty, desperately leafing through the tabloids, looking for things she didn't want to see. He hated his father for treating her like that, and he hated her for acting like that. Worst of all was the way they had to pretend that everything was fine, just fine, peachy keen fine.

At Christmas they would send out this schmaltzy picture of the three of them on the front lawn of the house, with their arms around each other like a happy family on daytime television. *Merry Christmas from the Nobles.* When he complained about it once, his father got angry.

"We're doing all this for you, Travis," he said.

Chapter

11

Letterkenny station was a cement platform under a rusting corrugated-iron roof, its three walls plastered with peeling posters. *The Bank of Ireland. Guinness is Good for You. Butlin's Holiday Tours*—a plump blonde in a pink bikini simpered on a tiny beach in front of a vaguely Mediterranean village. At one end of the platform a bus conductor in a black uniform sat on a dilapidated baggage cart and stared down at the damp floor. A cracked leather suitcase handle, torn off a bag long ago, stuck up through the wooden slats of the cart. Behind it, Sam and Hannah stood uncomfortably under a clock that had stopped permanently at eleven twenty-four one day.

"It's not exactly bustling," Hannah said. "Are you sure it's coming in at three o'clock?" She half hoped a mistake had been made. She half hoped he would never come and they could just drive back to Ballymarr, the two of them, and have some nice tea.

"I'm sure that's what the message said, but everything's late in Ireland." Sam hid his feelings very well, but she could hear a nervous quaver in his voice. Sometimes when he was anxious or irritated he pursed his lips slightly and then the muscle at the side of his jaw began its rhythmic clenching. Otherwise he held himself aloof from emotional display. She had never heard him raise his voice, and he had once told her that he hadn't cried since his father's death, when he was fourteen years old.

She fluffed at her hair and angled to get a look at her reflection in the glass of the ticket-seller's booth. She wanted to impress Travis with her sexy good looks and her calm, friendly manner. She wanted him to think that she was the right woman for Sam—at last. How would she compare with all those other girls of Sam's that Travis had met when he was younger? She wanted to win.

The red-and-white coach rounded a corner in the distance and came lumbering into view.

"He's not exactly traveling in style," Sam said.

"Maybe that's the only way to get here." She took Sam's hand but he didn't seem to notice. The old bus creaked in and lurched to a halt next to the platform. She searched for Travis's unknown face in the crowd with a mixture of anticipation and dread.

"Hey, isn't that him, Sam? Down at the end?"

It was hard to miss him in the mob of dark-suited Irishmen and women in flowered dresses with string bags. A rangy, all-American kid in a blue sweater, under a huge green backpack. He had his father's square jaw, beaky nose, and soft brown eyes, but he was made on a different scale. He seemed to be from another but closely related species in which each feature was larger and each gesture more emphatic. They were about the same height, but Sam gave the impression of being a much smaller man.

"Hi, Dad!" Travis grinned as he walked down the platform. He looked nervous, too, as he moved awkwardly to-

83

ward them under his load. Sam put out his hand and they shook hands.

"Hi, kiddo," he said. "This is Hannah Bart. My son, Travis." Hannah shook his hand and gave him her most appealing, sympathetic direct look. He didn't seem to notice.

"Here, let me give you a hand with that," Sam said. "Did you have a nice trip?"

The backpack was too big for the trunk, and Travis squeezed into the back seat next to it. He angled the pack so that the little monkey peeking out of the top didn't get crushed, and they took off into the Irish afternoon with Travis talking. He talked a lot. He told about the trip to Dublin and Donal O'Grady and his family and the train ride to Donegal, not pausing to wait for their reaction to one story before he started off on the next. Hannah began to relax. Maybe he was more nervous than she was. Too nervous to really notice her, probably, and certainly too nervous to make any judgments. Either that or he was the world's most compulsive nonstop storyteller. His logorrhea created a low, soporific drone. Sam smiled and laughed politely at the wheel as he babbled on. So far, so good.

When they got to Ballymarr, Travis bounded in through the hallway and up the staircase to his room without seeming to stop long enough to take in what a special place it was. They waited for him in the anglers' bar.

"He seems a little nervous," Hannah said.

"I think he looks great."

Travis appeared in the doorway. "Hey, this looks like a pretty ritzy place," he boomed across the room, coming over to flop into one of the big chairs.

"Would you like a whiskey, Travis?"

"Sure, Dad. Actually, I'd prefer a beer. They have really terrific beer in this country, have you noticed that? Thanks.

84

This place is terrific, it reminds me of something, though. Remember that place in Maine where we went a few times in the summer when I was a kid? We went fishing in a double-ended dory and I went out with the lobstermen a few times?"

Sam remembered. "Your mother didn't want you to go, but I thought you should have the experience," he said.

"Yeah, and remember when I came home with a couple of two-pounders from a pot I set and pulled myself? And Mom cooked them and the Brewsters came over and Mrs. Brewster brought homemade donuts?" The two men fell comfortably into reminding each other of the past, telling and retelling and embellishing. They talked about summer houses in Maine and cottages on Nantucket, and they talked about the furniture in the big house on 91st Street that had been sold after Nannou died, and they talked about the uncles and aunts and cousins who used to gather there for Thanksgiving and Christmas.

Travis told the story about the day the pig fell into the well at the family place in New Hampshire. Sam told how Great-great-great-grandfather Joshua Noble had been a barge captain on the Hudson River and how he had, very reluctantly, gone into business with his friend Commodore Vanderbilt—investing in a newfangled invention called the railroad.

Oft-told tales, worn by the generations to a comfortable, predictable litany, hummed in Hannah's ears. Both men had started to relax. These family stories were a formula, a familiar code for reestablishing communication between father and son. This way they avoided all the built-in embarrassment and awkwardness of meeting after so much anger. It was as if they were speaking another language—a male language. By this time two women would have gotten over their first discomfort and tackled the emotional subtext.

("I was disappointed when you left Southfield, but I can see how hard it was for you now.")

Privately, she recalled a few Bart family stories, stories that she and Jake and her parents had told each other over and over again. Were all family stories this reassuring for members of the family—and this boring for outsiders? Sometimes guests got a particular blank look on their faces when she and her family sat around the dining-room table talking about their own wonderful past, and now she understood why. A glaze of polite simulated attention settled over her features as Travis told how he had found a 'possum in the empty garbage pail behind the house in Ashmont one autumn weekend, and how, when prodding the soft gray animal with a stick got no response, and they were all convinced the 'possum was dead, they dumped it out of the pail and it ran off into the woods spitting and hissing.

"Remember that, Dad?"

Sam was laughing out loud, holding back nothing. She had never seen him laugh like that. They were on their third drink now, and Sam ordered their dinner to be brought to a table in the bar. Sam is happy, she thought. What's good for Sam is good for me and Sam. She resisted a powerful urge to bolt for her room as he swung into a story about the night Travis put a frog in his Cousin Albert's sleeping bag which-was-the-same-summer-wasn't-it that Marie the cook went into the laundry and found a porcupine in the washing machine and the men from the New Hampshire Fish and Game Department had to come and get it out?

"You were terrific with him, Sam, you guys really had a friendly time," she said later, when they were finally, finally alone in their bedroom.

"Wasn't that fun? I had forgotten what a family we were."

"You were pretty funny." Sam didn't seem to notice her boredom or her feeling of being left out at all. At the same

86

time, he was more physical and passionate with her than he had ever been.

"I love you, Hannah," he said. "I think you're wonderful. I never would have written Travis if you hadn't nagged me to." She was tired and dazed, but his ardor infected her and when they went to bed he took her roughly and surely, without waiting for her to come. With his arms around her, she fell into a confused sleep.

She dreamed that she was in Castle Tyrone with Hugh O'Neill, who looked like Frederick Culloden. He was about to leave. He would leave her there alone if she wasn't ready; she had to get packed. She had to be ready to go, she had to hurry. She needed to pack her suitcase but she was afraid to let him out of her sight. Already, she had forgotten things. What if he left without her? In the dream her anxiety grew as the night passed. Culloden stared out the window at the early Irish dawn.

And as she slept, dawn came again, revealing the brooding turrets of Ballymarr and the Erninmore below it, waking the potato farmers and sending the night animals back into their holes and hollow trees, and bringing a change in the weather.

The next day was as hot as an American day in July. By the time she got up, Sam had already organized and planned a picnic on the beach at Lough Swilly. Travis was waiting downstairs in his bathing suit and T-shirt, looking like a California beach boy.

"You look like a surfer," she said. But he was focused on Sam.

"Come on, Dad, let's go."

They drove down the rutted castle driveway toward the water, with Travis stretched out lengthwise in the back seat and Hannah clutching the hotel's straw picnic hamper on her lap in the front. The deserted white stretch of beach was bathed in green northern light, giving an eerie, gelatinous overtone to the noonday sun.

Across the glassy water the ruins of a gray stone fortress commanded a hill, and they could just pick out in the distance the remains of a chapel on the shore that had once provided spiritual comfort for its residents. Catholics. Celtic soldiers. Gaelic soldiers. Soldiers of the O'Neill chieftains. Beyond the fort, patches of farmland sloped down to the lough, which curved toward Dunaff Head and Fanad Head where they formed the rocky gateway to the stormy Atlantic. As they watched the water, a rainbow appeared in the spectral light, first a half-bow—a prism of colors bent over the water—and then an entire crescent forming and reforming in a perfect curve in the sky.

"Hey, look at that!" Travis whistled in appreciation and started down toward the edge of the beach to get closer to the ephemeral colors. The rainbow faded and she watched as Travis began searching for flat stones on the sand and skipping them. Four times. Seven times. Eleven times. One stone skimmed across the water in two great swoops and then floated in tiny bursts above the surface before finally disappearing. Travis was good at it. She turned to Sam.

"Travis sure is in a good mood," she said. "He seems fantastically cheerful."

"Well, what did you expect?" Sam smiled. Satisfaction, complacence.

"I don't know, I thought both of you would be very nervous about seeing each other again."

"I guess we were, but we got over it."

"At least you seem to have gotten over it."

"We're happy to see each other. Why shouldn't we be?"

"I guess I just expected more friction at first, more anger from him over what happened, or something like that."

Now Sam was smiling his manic smile. "Anger? At me?" He laughed. "How could anyone ever be angry at me?"

"Sam, don't you take *anything* seriously?" She threw a fistful of the grainy white sand at him, and he lunged back at her to try to intercept the launching of the second handful, and in a moment they were laughing and hugging each other. When Travis came back from the water's edge, she noticed that his face looked slightly out of kilter, as if something had upset him.

They settled down and she opened the hamper and passed out the beer. The hamper was elaborately fitted with thermoses, plates, and flatware for the kind of nineteenth-century picnic where men and ladies in their Sunday clothes sat on camp chairs and ate hot soups and puddings and pies. A stack of waxed-paper-wrapped sandwiches huddled in one corner.

"Looks good enough to eat," Travis said as she passed him one. He sat down on the sand facing her and started to unwrap it. The sun felt hot and she leaned back to pull off the white T-shirt she had on over her blue-and-white bikini. As she folded it, she looked up right into Travis's eyes. He didn't smile or say anything. And she suddenly wondered if he had been watching her while she pulled off her shirt, examining her body in the moments when she was helpless and blind as it slid over her head. She felt naked and exposed.

"Isn't this as beautiful as Colorado?" Sam asked, and Travis turned toward his father.

Hannah relaxed and dug her toes in the sand, reaching for the mysterious cool dampness below the surface. She imagined the sand, teeming with hidden creatures, extending down the shoreline and out under the water, making a soft glimmering floor for the clear green of the lough. The grains packed up between her toes and grated against the calluses on the soles of her feet. Maybe she should have a pedicure when they got back to New York.

"It sure is beautiful," Travis said.

"You don't miss all those snow-capped peaks?"

"I guess not," Travis said. And then: "I'm not sure if I'll go back there anyway."

"What would you do then?"

"I'm not sure."

"Any ideas—I mean, if you don't go back?"

"I don't know." Now Travis was digging his toes in the sand and looking uncomfortably down at his knees. "I thought maybe I'd come back to New York with you guys and maybe look for a job there or something. I could probably stay with Mom."

"I don't think *that* would be necessary, unless you preferred it," Sam said. He made this sound like a very unlikely possibility. "I would certainly be delighted to have you stay with me. There's plenty of room. And if you're interested, maybe I could do something about getting you a job somewhere in publishing."

"Gee, Dad, that would be great!" Travis was smiling now. Sam had said exactly what he wanted him to say. "I'm pretty sure I could even get my highschool degree if I took one of those exams they have; I almost had the credits when I left Bristol."

"We'll see what we can do," Sam said.

After lunch they walked a way down the beach. Water sparkled like distant jewels in the pockets of sand at the tide line as they headed north. Two tall figures and a smaller one arranging and rearranging themselves on the sand: Travis and Sam racing each other to a big live oak tree and coming back laughing and breathless; Sam and Hannah walking at the water's edge with their arms around each other, Travis a little behind them, looking for shells and pebbles; Hannah and Travis standing together on the shore giggling at Sam, up to his ankles but too cold to plunge in; Sam and Hannah on the shore watching Travis swim out and back toward them with a sure, crisp stroke. Travis and Sam and Sam and Hannah and Hannah and Travis.

Later Hannah packed up the remains of the picnic, folding the used waxed paper and putting the empty beer bottles back in the hamper. Sam picked up the towels they had left on the sand.

"I think I'd like to try and walk back to the hotel, if that's okay," Travis said. "I was talking to that guy, the head gillie, and he said there's a path from here along the river."

"Tired of being folded up like an accordion in the back of the car?" Sam said. "Okay, but be sure you make it back before eight o'clock. They serve dinner very promptly here. Make it seven-thirty to leave yourself time to get dressed."

"Sure, Dad, absolutely." Travis turned to go.

"Wait a minute. How are you going to tell what time it is?"

"Don't worry, Dad, I'll be there."

"The light is very deceptive here. Do you have a watch?"

"No." Travis had turned back toward them now and he exposed his naked wrists in a comic gesture. "No watch. Mom sent me one last Christmas, but it got broken before I came east."

"Well, here, take mine and don't be late for dinner. And don't break it, either." Sam unbuckled the leather strap from his wrist and handed Travis the flat gold watch with its onyx hands. Even Travis noticed how lovely it was; he cradled it in his palm.

"Hey, thanks, Dad, that's beautiful, I'll be very careful with it," he said, buckling it onto his wrist and heading down the beach. "Good luck getting it back!" He loped away along the shore, toward the trees, in his T-shirt and blue trunks. Long legs.

Hannah put the last of the empty bottles into the hamper

and closed the lid, bending over slowly and meticulously fastening the two straw latches. She slid the two wooden pegs through the wicker hoops at the outside of the basket and stood up.

"Here, let me take it." Sam picked the basket out of her hands and started to walk toward the car. She watched his elegant, unconcerned back in silence. His shirt was draped over one shoulder, covering half of the archipelago of raised white blotches where he had been wounded during the war. A souvenir of Manila, he called them. As she watched him, she willed herself to be silent, mature, patient, tough. Be magnificent, she reminded herself. But it was no use.

"Hey, I thought that was my watch," she said as they reached the car. "I thought it was mine." She tried to make her voice sound jokey and offhand. Sam stopped and put his arms into the sleeves of his shirt.

"It's getting chilly," he said.

"I thought that was my watch."

"Oh, sweetie, don't be angry about it. Of course it's your watch, I just loaned it to him."

"He said 'good luck getting it back.' I think he wants to keep it."

"Listen, don't worry so much. He's just a kid. If he keeps that one I'll get you an even better one." Sam put his arm around her shoulders and absentmindedly kissed the top of her right ear. "Hey, what do you think about him wanting to come and live in New York and get a job after all?" he said. "That's a switch."

His pleasure in Travis made her feel petty and childish. Of course he was right. Travis was just a kid and she was an adult and adults make allowances for kids. But in spite of herself she was hurt and sad. She missed the watch. It was her watch and she missed it. She missed the wonderful feeling she had had when she saw it on Sam's wrist and knew that it belonged to her—to them. She wanted *that* watch, she didn't want another newer, replacement watch. Why didn't Sam understand? She bit down on her jaw to keep herself from crying. If Sam had been watching her face, he could have seen her eyes fill up, but he was looking off into the distance over the lough.

"You know, I think having Travis here is going to bring us closer together," he was saying. "I feel a kind of unlocking inside me somewhere. I think I'm beginning to understand some of the things you've said. You were right, it was important for me to see him."

She blinked back the wetness on the surface of her pupils and felt a stinging around her eyes. If he saw her crying now, he might get upset and take back what he was saying. It would confuse him. But the knot in her stomach refused to untangle until they got back to the hotel and she escaped into the bathroom to get ready for dinner. It's all right, she silently crooned to herself, assessing her round face in the mirror above the sink. She would be magnificent, adult, in control. Travis had the watch. But she had Sam.

She walked down the staircase for dinner and playfully plucked the tops of the fly rods as she passed them on the landing. Travis and Sam were waiting for her at the table, crackling their menus and laughing about the possibilities. Behind them the river was bands of silver in the evening light, and the sounds of the water running past the terraces at the bottom of the gardens floated up through the still air. Travis was wearing the watch and it looked like a permanent fixture. He had adjusted the strap to fit his larger wrist. The old mark of the buckle was a dark scar on the soft brown leather.

Chapter

12

After breakfast Sam and Travis drove into Letterkenny to do some shopping. "Why don't you stay here and relax," Sam said. "That way we won't have to cram three into the car." Travis beamed as he slid into the passenger seat, her seat.

" 'Bye," she said. Now she was alone. Alone for the first time since she got off the plane at Shannon. A week ago she had been in New York. It seemed more like a month. She had a headache. Upstairs, she fished through her canvas sack for aspirin and bounced three of the white tablets into the palm of her hand. She found a glass in the bathroom and filled it with water. The pills tried to stick in her throat, but she swallowed hard and got them down. The bitter taste of aspirin stayed in her mouth. Maybe she would feel better if she went for a walk outside.

It was an overcast day and she walked slowly around the gardens in the flat, neutral light, following paths which wound between box hedges and yew hedges and listening to her heels click along the cobbled walks that went under a row of stone archways toward the stable yard.

She wandered through the kitchen garden: neat rows of beans and cabbages gleaming and fresh and innocently un- aware of their impending death by boiling. Below the vege- tables the path meandered into an arbor with long trellises of roses and borders of zinnias and pansies glowing red and purple and yellow against the dark soil.

A flight of steps led down to the water. Standing on the slab of stone at the bottom, she could look down through the pale-green depths of the river and see the fish. Near the rocks that lined the shore, a school of fingerlings darted back and forth. Beyond them, two trout, one behind the other, swam lazily upstream along the bottom. Hannah watched them for a long time.

If Travis was going to live in New York and get a job, he would stay at Sam's apartment. There wouldn't be any point in his going to the trouble of finding his own. Sam wouldn't want him to, there was plenty of room at his place. Travis would be with them all the time. He was going to stay with them now, on her vacation. That's what he'd said. "I thought maybe I'd come back to New York with you. . . ." Their plans for traveling around Ireland would now be plans for three people instead of plans for a couple falling in love. How would she fit into this triangle? She wouldn't be Sam's girl traveling romantically alone with him any more, but she wouldn't be Travis's mother either. Or even Sam's wife. Maybe she should just go home where she belonged.

Before, when she had had stepchildren she had at least been their official stepmother. Joe's wife. Not that it made any difference. She had ended up feeling just as hurt and left out as she did now.

"You'll never be their real mother," the psychiatrist said. "But when you married this man you married his children."

"He has to decide who's more important. Them . . . or us."

"He can't make that choice and you can't ask him to," the *psychiatrist said.*

She sat down on the step. The coldness of the stone seeped through the fabric of her jeans. Why did everything have to be so complicated? If you protest and complain about other people's children, that makes you a selfish old maid. But if you don't protest, your anger pools inside you. You are choked by it. You drown. Either way, you are the outcast, the one who doesn't belong. A man with his children is a sacred sight, hallowed by nature, smiled on by society. They belong to each other forever.

"You shouldn't try to come between a man and his children," the *psychiatrist said. "You'll understand when you have children of your own."*

If she had children of her own. Sam hadn't gotten anywhere near the subject of marriage, much less children. Why would he? He was having enough trouble dealing with the one he already had. And time was passing. Thirty. She was already older than the gynecologist had said she should be the first time she asked back in Illinois. Now her New York doctor said she had at least five years, but even five years was a limited time.

Five years? You have sixty more shots at it, a friend had said. And now she was beginning to think that way too. Each month was one shot less, one egg less, a great big X on the calendar of her childbearing years. She longed for the kind of acceptance that mothers get. The sappy smiles on people's faces when they passed you on the street, the instant legitimacy, the instant respect. For now she was a mistress, the lowest rung on the totem pole, under mother and under wife and way, way under son. In New York, Travis and Sam would be a family, and she would be just another one of Sam's girls. Oh, yes, isn't she the one he went to Ireland with?

She walked back toward the castle.

Sam and Travis were stumbling into the hall with their arms full of packages, laughing and talking. There was a new plaid-flannel shirt and new red socks for Travis. There were new matching green fishing caps for Sam and Travis and new bandannas for Sam. There was a fly box for Sam and shoelaces for Travis. There was nothing for Hannah.

"I'm really wiped out. I guess the trip up from Paris is catching up with me," Travis said, stretching his long frame in one of the big chairs after lunch. "I think I'll go and take a nap, if that's permitted here at Camp Noble."

"Sure, kiddo, I understand. You're just getting too old to hack it," Sam teased him. "You'd better rest up for the fishing. I'm going to walk down to the river and see if I can find that flashlight I lost the other night."

They walked together in silence down the gravel driveway. Hannah scuffed at the loose pebbles with her sandals. Sam was humming to himself as they turned into the arch that led to the river paths.

"In a bar on the Piccola Marina," he sang under his breath in a bright English accent, "life called to Mrs. Wentworth Breeewstah,/fate beckoned her and introduced her,/into a rather queer/unfamiliar atmosphere." Sam loved to sing Noel Coward songs, and he knew the words to almost all of them. As they walked along the path she kept her head low, hiding her face.

It was Sam who found the flashlight—a silver cylinder sparkling in a clump of prickly green furze near where he had been casting. She looked down the river and remembered that night. They had been alone together. She had been so happy.

"Now what's the matter, sweetie?" Sam said.

"Nothing."

He stood blocking the pathway in front of her. His soft flannel shirt was tucked into deep-brown corduroys and the flashlight was already neatly stowed in one pocket. A gleaming leather belt crossed his lean torso. She felt dowdy.

"Really, it's not important."

"Come on, now." Gently, as if she were a little girl, he lifted a tendril of hair away from her face and tucked it behind her right ear. "This is your vacation and you're not having any fun. What is it, sweetie? Tell me."

"It's no big deal, I'm probably just being silly."

His tenderness thawed her resolve. She wanted to collapse in his arms, to crumble and cry, to confess everything and let him find the answers. Fat, betraying tears welled up in her eyes. She hated tears. She hated the disadvantage of being the one who always cried. Sam never cried.

"It's just that being with you and Travis is a lot different from being alone with you." She tried to sound cool and reasonable, but her voice was husky and cracked. "I mean, he's a terrific kid and it's so great that you're together again, but I guess it makes me feel kind of lonesome."

"But you shouldn't be upset, sweetie. You know I have to concentrate on Travis for a while. I have to make up for lost time, you know that."

"It's not that I don't understand—I do," she said. "It's just that I miss our time together. I don't know, I was having such a good vacation before he came." Her voice dipped into tears.

"Now tell me, because I'm confused about this." Sam drew away and let his voice get earnest and concerned. "I thought you *wanted* me to get back on good terms with Travis, didn't you? After all, it was *your* idea."

"I know, I know, I'm just being silly." Black discouragement engulfed her. Sam would never understand. Even she didn't really understand. She gave up and buried her head in the softness of his shirt. Her face crumpled and she sobbed against his chest.

"There, there," he said, comforting her and stroking her back. "I guess this whole situation is a little upsetting for all of us. There, there. Come on, why don't we have some time to ourselves this afternoon, okay? It's true, we haven't had much time together since Trav came. Let's go on in and go back to bed and have a little snuggle and a talk and work this out, hmmmm?"

They started back along the path with their arms locked around each other. She kicked against the pebbles again and smiled through her dried tears.

"I can see that it's hard for both of you," Sam said. "You're both here to be with me, and you can't both have me at the same time." Smug, but she let it pass. He was trying. And for the moment, right now, he was hers. He was with her and they were going to make love and get close again and talk and work something out so that she would feel better. For a while at least it would be as if Travis had never come. Better. Travis could go take a flying fuck with his little-boy jealousies and his boring stories. She hoped he was having a nice nap.

She put an arm around Sam's waist from behind and hooked her thumb over the edge of his belt, rubbing her body against him as they walked. He played her game, laughing as he tried to stay in mincing step with her smaller strides, and exaggerating the difference between the lengths of their legs.

"Wait until I get those tiny limbs of yours upstairs," he said, and he stopped for a minute, turning his body in front of her for an embrace.

Over Sam's shoulder she saw Travis. He was standing

above them at the head of the driveway. He must have been watching them since they came through the stone arch from the river. His face was stern, his eyes blank and angry. The expression struck her chest like a blow; she felt for a moment like a silly child caught at a frivolous game. But Sam wasn't intimidated, or else he didn't notice.

"Hi there, Trav," he called out blithely. "What happened to your nap? Have an attack of insomnia?"

Travis didn't laugh. His lips looked thin and white as if he were pressing them together, and the skin on his face seemed to be pulled tight against the bones of the skull.

"I came after you guys, but I guess you didn't want company," he said.

Hannah waited for Sam to stick up for himself. He would explain to Travis that he and Hannah were on their way up for a nap. He would say that he wanted to be alone with her sometimes. He would tell Travis to knock it off.

"We were looking for the flashlight," Sam said. "You were welcome to come along."

"I guess it's just as well I didn't," Travis said, letting his eyes rest on their locked arms. "If you have a minute to spare for me, Dad, I wonder if you could come up to my room. There's something I'd like to show you." His tone implied that Sam rarely had a minute to spare for him.

"Sure, kiddo, let's go," Sam said. He gave Hannah's arm a last squeeze and disappeared up the driveway and into the castle, following Travis's unyielding back without question.

Hannah walked up to the terrace and sat down heavily on one of the stone benches. Shit. A wave of longing for her own friends and her own apartment and her own life in New York choked her and made her feel like crying again. She certainly didn't want to stay here and compete with Travis. Especially not if he was going to win. Maybe she should just go home and let them be together. Maybe she should just give up and go home.

She thought about her bedroom with its comforter, and the way the sun came into the room in the late afternoon. Home. Her office, the bulletin board, and the big poster of the Illinois prairie that she sometimes felt she could walk right into. Home. Would David have found another girl? Or would he still be waiting for her? It had only been a week, really, and he must have known that this would happen. David was the man she belonged with after all. He was like her, young and always hoping for better things. No fancy restaurants, no sports cars, no fittings at a London tailor.

How could she have thought that those things were important? How could she have thought she could belong in Sam's world? He was an old man, an old man with a lot of unresolved problems. She wanted to go home.

But she knew that if she tried to leave now there would be trouble and scenes. Sam would want an explanation. He wouldn't understand. Why couldn't they all have a good time together, he would want to know. Weren't they all having a good time together? If she left now, she would be the sorehead, the troublemaker, the one who couldn't take it.

The chill from the stone bench made her back ache. Shadows were spilling early darkness into the cracks between the flagstones on the terrace, and the river suddenly looked sinister and mysterious in the twilit distance. After a while she got up and walked back to the front door of the castle.

She went inside and through the dark hall. Sam and Travis were in the library, chatting happily over their afternoon tea.

"Oh, Hannah," Sam said cheerfully, "come on in and have some tea, it's chilly out there." It was as if the earlier part of the afternoon had never happened.

"What did Travis want to show you?" she said.

"Oh, he just wanted to ask about some of the flies we bought in town today, the March Browns—right, Trav? Milk or lemon, sweetie?"

She sank into the warmth of the deep chair and focused on that moment of physical comfort. She would be magnificent. She would be above it all. She would hang on at least until Jake got there. He would be on her side, and with him here she would be able to figure out what to do. She could handle it. She wasn't going to let some sulky, overgrown teenager ruin her vacation and her affair with Sam.

"Lemon, please," she said. "Thanks, Sam." She reached out and touched his arm as he handed her the cup. That would annoy Travis. Then she leaned back in the chair and concentrated on being charming and sexy and pleasing. She would dazzle Sam, and later he would be sorry he had lost her. She willed a hard and polished surface to form around her real feelings.

Chapter
13

Hannah woke up slowly, pulling herself out of the heavy depths of sleep. It was dark. The indistinct shapes of the chairs and bedside table loomed against the faint light from the windows. The headache was back. Aspirin.

She slipped out from under the covers, trying not to jostle Sam's body, and walked across the room to the door. There was no one in the hall at this hour; she could make it to the bathroom without a robe. She stepped out and shut the bedroom door behind her. Suddenly she felt dizzy. She took a few more steps toward the bathroom and the pain in her head began to spin. Her knees buckled, a sickening cloud of night poured from some inner part of her brain.

Later she opened her eyes. There was a rough wool carpet under her back, but it was too dark to see anything. Her skin was covered with sweat and she shivered in a night draft. Slowly she turned over and propped her torso up on her hands and knees. If she stood up straight, she might lose her balance or hit her head. Her mouth tasted of rust and salt, and her legs throbbed with fresh pain. Beads of perspiration dripped down the insides of her arms as she crawled ahead in the pitch black, reaching out with her hands to feel for obstacles and clues with each step. The darkness was complete. Where was she? Maybe she was on the rug in the living room of her apartment. No, it was never this dark there. Maybe she was in the basement room of her parents' house, but that room wasn't carpeted.

A wall materialized out of the darkness about a foot in front of her and she reached up toward it. There was an angle, she was kneeling in a corner. Slowly she stood up and leaned against the wall for support as she walked along it to the right, step, step, carefully feeling her way with both palms flat. She was hot now; in spite of the darkness her nakedness made her feel dangerously vulnerable and exposed. Finally in the middle of the wall there was a light switch, a familiar lever embedded in a metal plate.

The lights blinded her at first. She looked around as her eyes adjusted to the glare. She was on the landing of a big staircase, the staircase at Ballymarr. She remembered now. Ireland, she was in Ireland.

She walked up the stairs and back into the bathroom, supporting herself against the wall. Shutting the door behind her, she sat on the edge of the tub and hung her head down between her knees until she felt steady again. Then she got up and sponged off her skinned knees with warm water. That's better. Her head began to clear and fear ebbed out of the angles of her nerves.

She must have fainted. She must have fainted on the way to the bathroom and fallen down the stairs. That's right. At dinner she had eaten very little and had too much wine. The tension in her head had kept her from being hungry, and Sam had looked at her approvingly when she passed up bread and dessert. No wonder she was so shaky. Just an accident. That's what the doctor had said once before when she fainted in the kitchen after a dinner party for Joe's parents. Something about the vagus nerve. Just an accident.

She found the bottle of aspirin in the cabinet and swallowed three. She would be okay now. She left the bathroom light on and walked by its glow back across the hall, noticing for the first time how treacherously close the stairs were. Quietly, trying not to disturb him, she lay down next to Sam. The throbbing in her knees was fading. His regular breathing relaxed her and she reached over to touch his back, running her hand lightly over the scars on his shoulder. He murmured a contented endearment in his sleep. Sweet Sam. She curled up next to him and slept again.

In the morning, the night's terror seemed like a distant dream. She wouldn't say anything about it. Sam probably wouldn't understand it and it would just upset him and make him ask questions. When he asked about her skinned knees, she feigned surprise.

"Oh, I guess I must have slipped on the rocks when we were fishing the other day," she said. "Did I have those scabs yesterday?" He didn't remember.

"Poor baby," he said. "Do they hurt?"

"Not really." And that was the end of it.

At breakfast Hannah ordered tea instead of coffee. The doctor had told her to avoid caffeine or liquor if she felt nervous.

"That's a good idea," Sam said, and he ordered tea, too. Sam loved anything that seemed elegant or unusual, and she laughed to herself about how confused he would be if he knew the real reason she wanted tea.

They were finishing breakfast when one of the waitresses came over to their table to say that there was a long-distance telephone call for Hannah. It had to be Jake! As she left the table a rush of adrenaline made her feel light-headed and giggly. Help was coming. She imagined a brigade of cavalry in their blue-and-gold uniforms tootling their bugles as they galloped over the ridge to rescue the besieged settlers in the stockade.

The old-fashioned telephone was bolted to the wall, and she had to stand on tiptoe to talk into the mouthpiece.

"I'm in Donegal now," Jake said. She could barely hear him over the scratch and static of the machinery inside the wires. "There's a bus to Letterkenny in about an hour if you two lovebirds are still interested in having me pay you a visit."

"Wonderful," Hannah yelled into the mouthpiece. "Don't worry about interrupting anything. Travis is already here." Her voice sounded unhappy and sarcastic, and she realized how loud it was. Was Travis behind her somewhere in the hallway, listening?

"Okay, I'm on my way," Jake shouted. "See you later."

"Great," she said. "I can't wait to see you." But the line had gone dead. She wondered if Jake had hung up or if the faltering machinery had finally failed. At any rate, he was coming. Nothing could stop him now.

Hannah stood on the cement bus platform, imagining Jake's friendly form swinging down the steps of the battered old coach. The little car was parked outside, out of sight. She was aware at some level that Jake would make a joke about the car, and she wanted to delay that joke.

Jake had always been the sobersides, the one who disapproved of frivolity and ostentation. He was the kind of person who read the front pages of the newspaper more carefully than the sports section, and who took the unemployment rate and the inflation percentages seriously. He never watched television. She looked around nervously at the dingy bus station, noticing the grimy scraps of newspaper heaped in the corners. She hoped Jake's neatness wouldn't be so put off by the bus and the station that he would be feeling negative about the whole thing before they even got to Ballymarr. She needed him. She needed him to be in a good mood.

In a lot of ways Jake and Travis were opposites. Jake had had a hard time in school because he was uncoordinated and unpopular although he got straight A's. Unlike Travis, he had made up his mind to overcome his handicaps. And he had done it, too, slowly winning the respect of his classmates through hard work and sharing what he had. He had graduated with honors from Exeter, but his great victory was a letter in soccer—even though everyone knew it had been awarded more for spunk and sportsmanship than for any athletic ability.

Now at Harvard he was a rising star on the *Crimson* and a member of the Signet already. His struggle had left him with a cautiousness about people his own age, but he had come through with a kind of polished toughness that reminded her of Sam sometimes. You never knew what Jake was really thinking.

The battered red-and-white coach pulled around the corner and drew up to the platform. Jake got off, clumsily shouldering his backpack in a way that made it bump against both sides of the doorway and the people standing behind him. He turned and mumbled an apology.

"Hey, Jake!" she welcomed him. "Am I ever glad to see you." She wanted to hug him, but they shook hands.

"Here, let me help you with that," she said.

Jake whistled when he saw the Alfa. She knew he would.

"That's a lotta car!" he said. "Is this what the famous Sam Noble is really like?" He didn't sound friendly.

"Well—" She found herself hesitating to defend Sam. "It's great for these narrow Irish roads. I mean, if you're going to drive a lot, it makes sense to have a good car." It sounded silly.

"It makes sense?" Jake smiled. "Would you like to try that one again?"

She laughed. "Come on, it's here so let's enjoy it," she said, as she squeezed his pack into the back seat. "It's not Sam's fault that he's rich."

"Listen to the new philanthropy. And here I always

thought you considered it unfair that Dad didn't have the money for you to go to Stanford."

It was true. Hannah had never been able to win scholarships the way Jake did, but she had been so proud and pleased when she got into Stanford. Her first choice! Then there was that awful talk with her father and the look on his face when he had to explain that Stanford was too expensive and too far away. In the end her father's obvious anguish over the situation had made her feel almost guilty about getting into Stanford in the first place. Instead, she had gone to the University of Chicago. But Jake was wrong; after the decision was made she had never felt angry about it. She never thought about it at all. Her life had gone on at Chicago and she never stopped to wonder what it would have been like if she had been somewhere else.

"God, it's great to see you," she said. "I've been miserable without anyone to remind me how miserable I was."

Jake leaned over and kissed her. "Hi, Hannah," he said. "Nice to see you. Let's start all over again and I'll try not to be so testy."

Driving through the narrow gray streets of Letterkenny, she began to relax. Her brother was beside her. Muscles loosened, nerves tingled across her back. It felt as if she had been holding her breath for days. Sometimes she had the same feeling after a plane landed. As it sat safely on the runway, her whole body would begin to unclench, and it was only then that she allowed herself to realize how tense she had been while it was in the air. Now she teased Jake, chattering away and confiding in him without having to weigh her words. She was light and breezy again and in control.

"How's old Travis doing?" Jake asked.

"Okay, I guess, for him."

Jake laughed. "I figured he'd give you some trouble," he

said. "He was pretty wild in Paris when we were there. I got the feeling he didn't like me much."

"I don't think he likes anyone who gets in the way of his relationship with his father."

"Yeah, that's what I thought, too. He's pretty stuck on Sam Noble and the famous Noble family and the great Noble family publishing house. The minute anyone brought up the subject of his trip to Ireland he'd begin to point like a bird dog. He couldn't wait to start north without me. God, once someone at the hostel made a nasty remark about Wasps and gentlemen in publishing, and I thought Travis was going to kill him. The poor guy didn't even know who Travis's father was—but he found out, all right. Is he still that tense?"

"He sure is. It's like competing with another woman for Sam's attention all the time."

"It's that bad?"

"Oh, Jake, it's worse than that bad. Travis is a complete baby and I guess Sam feels so guilty about him that he caters to it. Most of the time it's as though I'm not even there, but when Travis does notice me I have the feeling that he'd like to kill me for being with his father." Her feelings rushed out in a pure blast of words.

"Come on, Hannah, you shouldn't get so upset. He's just a kid." She had forgotten that Jake didn't approve of emotional outbursts. "After all, he hasn't seen his father for years. He's got a lot to be jealous about."

"Well, that's *tough*. His terrible, terrible childhood is over and he's with his father now. In fact, it was because I practically forced him to that Sam invited him in the first place. What thanks do I get? Zero. He's so involved in acting like Young Werther that he doesn't even stop to think how this came about."

"It's true, he is a little melodramatic," Jake said. He had assessed the force of her anger and decided not to try to reason with her. "He's pretty messed up about a lot of things, and it's worse because he can be so charming that he gets away with it." Jake had a way of talking about his peers as if they were much younger than he was. "In Paris, he was able to make friends with almost everyone. Metro conductors, cops, waitresses. We hardly ever saw him because he was always off with this or that French friend that he had met somewhere. You know it's not that easy to meet French people, either. It's not as if he spoke any French."

"Listen, I can see how charming and open he is. I even like him in a way. It's just that he wants to have Sam to himself. He wishes I didn't exist, and that's a little rough for me."

"Doesn't Sam help you out?"

She shrugged. "Not much. It's hard for him to deny Travis anything right now."

"Well, maybe he'll catch on."

"God, I hope so."

They were quiet for a minute. Jake looked out the window at the empty green landscape whizzing by. "You should have seen Travis operate in Paris, though," he said finally. "He really got on some people's nerves. There was this terrific girl at the hostel, Helen Johnson, and Travis drove her crazy."

She could tell that Jake had brought this up because he wanted to talk about the girl. "What was she like?" she obliged. "What did Travis do to *her?*"

"Well, Helen is really uptight about her French, I guess because she's studied it a lot," Jake said. "I mean, she was so proud about it that she would go hungry sometimes rather than try to ask for something she didn't know the words for. I kept telling her how silly it was, but I guess that's just the way she is." It sounded as if the way she was was all right with Jake.

"It does sound kind of silly. Did you know her from before?"

"No. It's funny, I didn't, but she goes to M.I.T., right across the river, and it turns out her brother was at Exeter with me."

"How did Travis drive her crazy?" Jake wanted to talk about Helen, but she wanted to talk about Travis.

"Oh, Travis thought she was very snooty. We'd go somewhere together and she would speak her perfect French, but he would just interrupt her even though he didn't know any French. He would point at things on the shelves or use grunts or sign language—communicating any way he could. Helen would sit there and cringe and pretend we weren't together. She called him the gorilla."

"I'm surprised he didn't kill her for that."

"No, he seemed to kind of like it. He was pretty easygoing about everything, except his father. It was as if he was happy to be different from us, even though he hung around all the time."

"Is Helen going to stay in Paris?"

"Yeah. Well, maybe. She said she'd wait for me to come back, although I'm not at all sure that she will. I'll see her in the fall anyway if she wants to see me. She certainly was glad to see Travis leave, though, I can tell you that."

"How did she feel when you left?"

"Oh." Jake smiled. "I guess she was a little pissed off."

"You didn't have to come, you know."

"Come off it, Hannah. I wanted to come." Jake reached out and shook her by the shoulder. "Don't worry about Helen. It's no big deal, she's just a friend."

"I'm sorry, I guess I'm still tense."

"Well, you can relax now, Jake is here," he said. And they were both laughing as the car swept up the gravel driveway to Ballymarr.

Chapter

14

At dinner Jake and Travis compared their trips north from Paris. It sounded like a friendly conversation: Jake's measured judgments and terse descriptions, Travis's explosive opinions and rambling accounts of people he had met and sights he had seen. There was an edge to their talk when they described their time in Paris, but it didn't seem sharp—or dangerous. Jake told how Travis had consumed so much Bordeaux at a genteel student wine-tasting party that he had to be carried home. Travis laughed. And Travis reported that Jake habitually slept until two in the afternoon and was known to his friends as Rip, for Rip Van Winkle. Jake laughed.

They both complained about the French professor from Williams who was in charge of the hostel for the summer. Travis thought he was uptight. Jake thought he was incompetent. Through the window of the dining room Hannah could see the curves of the Erninmore glimmering and darkening. Maybe this is going to be all right. Jake and Travis will be the kids together, and Sam and I will be the grown-ups.

She twisted her neck to look around the dining room at the other guests. The trysting couple was gone. With a prurient sadness, she thought of them each returning to their happy spouses and contented children. What would happen now? Would the betrayed husband and wife go on forever in complacent innocence? Or did they have lovers of their own? The young German had been joined by a friend who looked so much like him that she thought they might be brothers. They sat in the opposite corner. The elegant man eating alone was gone, and a sleek dark-haired family dominated the center of the room. A slender olive-skinned woman in a brown silk dress with two strands of pearls was speaking to her children in mellifluous Italian.

"Babbo viene domani," she told them. Your father will be here tomorrow.

"I've never been to Ireland," Jake was saying to Sam. "What made you decide to come here?"

"I had heard about Ballymarr," Sam said. "I had to be in London, so it seemed like a convenient place to gather." He grinned with male complicity at Jake. "Anyway," he said, "I thought it was about time someone taught your sister a proper sport like fly fishing."

Jake laughed. "She always liked to fish," he said. "I just don't remember her actually catching anything."

"Well, I did here, didn't I, Sam?" she said. "You just didn't notice all the fish I caught," she teased Jake. "You were too busy reading to notice."

"Sure," Jake said. "And you're always so timid about your accomplishments, so quiet and low key."

"Well, I thought at least that teaching her to fish would be a nice rest for the fish," Sam laughed with Jake. "Nobody ever thinks of the fish."

Hannah looked over at Travis, intending to tease him about his lack of experience too. She tried to catch his eye, but he was staring across the room. When he noticed that she was looking at him, he pushed his chair away from the table and stood up.

"I think I'll go take a walk," he said.

"What is it, Trav?" Sam snapped out of his laughter and into fatherly concern. "Did you eat something bad?"

"No, I'm okay."

"Don't you want to wait and have coffee with us?"

"No." Travis walked out of the dining room with a worried Sam in his wake. She couldn't help gloating as she watched them disappear through the doorway. For once Travis was acting like the sorehead. She was winning at last.

"Come on, let's go have coffee in the other room," she said. The waitress brought them coffee in a white porcelain pot and she poured it into two cups. The coffee was weak and brackish, but it made her head feel clear and her heart beat a little faster.

"See what I mean about Travis?"

"Yes, I see what you mean," Jake said. "It must be hard for him, though, having to share his father with you after all this time."

"Too bad," she said. But when Sam came back into the room looking confused and old, her heart softened.

"Is he okay?"

"Oh, sure. I think he just got bored."

"Would you like some coffee?"

"How is it?"

"The usual," she said. She meant this as a joke, but Travis's mood stayed with them. Uncomfortable chatter. If she had been alone with Jake, they would have talked about Travis. If she had been alone with Sam, they would have avoided talking about Travis.

Jake talked a little about the living arrangements at Harvard. Sam told him about the fraternities at Williams back when he was there.

"I suppose it's very different now," he said.

"Well, the clubs aren't as important, but some things haven't changed much," Jake said. "It's still amazing how much athletic prowess counts for in a place like Harvard." Jake loved to complain about the low mental abilities of his classmates who were on athletic scholarships, the guys who were nothing but jocks. It made him feel better about his own lack of coordination.

"I'll bet no one ever got a fly-casting scholarship," Hannah said.

"I don't know, there was a guy at Haverford I heard about who got a tennis scholarship," Jake said. "I mean, tennis!"

"Do you play tennis?" Sam asked.

"Sure," Hannah said. "Not in your league, though."

"Maybe the four of us should try some doubles tomorrow," Sam said. "Fred Culloden has a court over at Castle Tyrone and he invited me to use it while we're here. I noticed that he is inordinately proud of it. It's probably pretty bumpy, but I would guess it's one of Ireland's few tennis courts."

"Why not?" Hannah said. "Can we borrow rackets?"

"Sure."

And after a while they went upstairs to bed.

They put the top down on the car the next morning after breakfast and the two boys sat up on the back seat in the wind. The green murkiness of the air around the lough made the morning seem timeless. In the Eastern part of the sky, the light from the rising sun was dispelled by the heavy atmosphere into a low-watt glow.

"Frederick's away," Sam said. "I called this morning. I'm sorry you won't get to meet him, Travis. I talked to the housekeeper and she insisted we come and use the court anyway."

Hannah turned around. "The castle has a pretty interesting history," she said to Jake. He leaned forward to hear her as she quickly retold what she remembered of O'Neill's dilemma and the Flight of the Earls.

"What happened after that?" Jake asked.

"Well, after he took off, there was Plantation, you know, and the English under James came in and resettled all this land with Scottish and Dutch Protestants."

Travis leaned forward suddenly, pushing his face toward hers. She had thought he wasn't listening.

"You mean that old guy just took off and left his son and everyone?" he asked.

"I guess that's right," she said.

"It's just history," Jake said. "If he had stayed, it probably wouldn't have changed things anyway."

"At least he would have been there. At least he wouldn't have just chickened out," Travis said. Suddenly he sounded really angry.

Sam turned around as if Travis's tone had reached out and hooked him by the ear. "Sometimes people can't help it, Trav," he said in a gentle, cajoling voice. "It's just the way sometimes you have to leave your children for a while rather than live with a woman you don't love any more. Sometimes you have to put your own life first, no matter how hard it is. You can't just decide to sacrifice yourself and be a saint about it unless there's a very good reason."

"A child is a good reason," Travis said.

15

The wind blurred the sound of Travis's voice as Sam guided the car north, and Sam wasn't sure what either of the boys was saying. Maybe talking to Jake would calm Travis down. After Letterkenny he took the left turn and then the smaller road off to the right. The housekeeper had offered him directions, but he didn't need them. He was pretty damn good at remembering places and routes even when he had only been on them once.

As they climbed the hills above the lough he noticed horses grazing in the fields that weren't given over to farming. They looked scrawny and weak. Bred for racing, but bred to lose. Two years ago he had gone to the Dublin Horse Show in July and then to the races at Ballybritt in Galway. What a joke! The start for the horses was a tape instead of a starting gate. The jockey on the favorite lost his horse in the opening parade and had to go racing around the track after it in a Rover. Primitive. He had kept his money in his pocket in spite of the picturesque squawking of the ring of carpet-baggers. How could you bet at a track like that?

At least Frederick had the good sense to spend his money on the things the Irish were good at: gardens and fishing waters and paintings and servants in livery. They drove through the white cast-iron gates into the splendid colors of the castle's lower fields of flowers, speckled like a pointilliste painting in the pale sun. *La Grande Jatte.* The monkey on a leash. As he turned away from the castle toward the tennis court there were camellia and fuchsia blossoms nodding over the edge of a velvety lawn, set like a lake among the trees. Copper beeches glowed above a broad flagstone terrace planted carefully with the design of a thumb and five fingers in blazing red coleus. The Red Hand of Ulster, the bloody Irish.

Beyond the gardens the pink rectangle of a tennis court stood out like a wound against the gray moors. Sam had played on a lot of tennis courts: Coral Beach in Bermuda and the River Club in New York and the grass courts at the Maidstone Club in East Hampton. But he had to admit that this court of Frederick's had a gallant charm all its own. It was rolled clay, not asphalt or Har-Tru or any of the surfaces which would have been a thousand times more convenient, especially in the Irish climate.

Next to it, an impeccable stone copy of a corbeled shepherd's hut was stocked with rackets, unopened cans of Slazengers, and even a stack of fresh towels embroidered with a pale-blue C. Frederick certainly knew how to do things, even if his taste was a little effeminate. He had mastered the texture of life with a grace that made his skill seem effortless, natural, inherent. Sam remembered sailing past the wooden towers of the Culloden summerhouse, tucked among the pines and rocks on their private island off Vinalhaven. He remembered the gleaming steps and banisters of their house on Beacon Hill, and he was filled with nostalgia and admiration.

They tested the grips on the array of rackets lined up in racks inside the hut. Sam opened the gate around the court and led the way out onto the pink, springy clay. Could Hannah and Jake play at all? He hoped he'd get a passable game out of this, at least.

"Why don't you come over and play the first set with me, Travis?" he said, as he passed around the net. He tested its height by putting his racket vertically and then horizontally against it. Perfect.

"Sure, Dad." Travis pranced over to the far side of the net to join his father. "It's the Noble team against the Bart team. Let's go!"

Through the netting, Sam saw Hannah and Jake give each other a look of mock alarm, sharing a private reaction. Did Hannah and Jake talk about him when he wasn't around? Did she tell Jake things that he didn't know about? Sometimes he wished *he* had had a brother.

The warm-up was inconclusive. Sam and Jake rallied on one side of the court while Hannah and Travis hit another ball back and forth on the opposite side. Jake was concentrating on the game and trying very hard, but Sam couldn't tell if he was rusty or clumsy. Out of the corner of his vision he saw Hannah get off a couple of good strong forehands; next to him, Travis was hitting the ball very hard and missing the court a lot.

"Ladies first," Sam said.

"First one in?" she pleaded with him, cocking her head like a little girl. Cute.

"Sure." He nodded back at her and bent down slightly for the serve, standing in front of the baseline because he didn't expect a strong one. Her first two tries were straight but too long. Her third was an ace. It angled fast across the court and caught him by surprise. A miss. He watched her change places with Jake and steady herself for her serve to Travis.

There was a lot of masculine strength in that cute little girl. Her serve was certainly a shock; her father must have taught her how to play. He was expecting one of those slow, high, pussycat serves most women learn at school. She was playing well, and it pleased him to miss an occasional shot of hers, especially when she came up to the net. She needed the encouragement, and he was good enough to give it to her.

In fact, he was very good. He knew it, although he never said it himself. "I play a fairly steady game," he would say, if anyone asked. Smoking slowed him down a bit, though, and he hadn't worked out at the club gym since he left New York six weeks ago. He liked to keep himself in regular trim with calisthenics and bench work. He loved the lean, purified feeling it gave him, and the steam room afterward, with the faces of his old friends and classmates framed in white clouds like the angels in *settecento* paintings.

He didn't want to think about his looks. He was always careful to avoid his own reflection in mirrors or store windows, and he never examined himself for muscle development after workouts the way some of the men did. Male vanity was unhealthy and it led to softness, womanliness. Vanity was for women. It was a wonderful thing, too, to watch a beautiful woman in front of a mirror. Gazing intently into her own face with a toss of the head, a slight correction of her makeup, the straightening of an earring. He loved beautiful women, but he was afraid of them as well.

Or maybe he was just tired of them. Tired of the trouble, the hysterics, the pretty sulks and then the real, ugly sulks. Was it bad luck that they all ended up clinging to him and collapsing in his apartment and begging him to let them stay? Leeches. They wanted to get him, to trap him and tie him down, to make him as weak as they were. Maybe Hannah was a change in the pattern. Her serve was certainly a change.

Now she served a low hard ball to Travis. He was ready and slanted the ball back across Jake's court into the alley. Jake was standing too far back and he missed it. When she served to Sam this time he returned the ball squarely to Jake's forehand, and Jake lobbed a high soft shot to Travis. A mistake. Travis danced up to the ball, lifted his racket in perfect, gleeful anticipation, and spun an unreturnable shot across the baseline.

"Hurrah!" he shouted, jumping up in a self-congratulatory cheer.

Seeing her through the pattern of the net, under the white tape along the top, Sam remembered the first time he had met Hannah. In fact, he hadn't even noticed her. It was at a publication party for one of his authors, and he knew that even if he *had* noticed her, he wouldn't have been very impressed. She was healthy-looking but not particularly pretty, and publicists weren't his favorite people in the business anyway. Women in public relations—or public affairs, or the information office, or whatever they liked to call it— were usually a little too plain and a little too eager. They had a kind of desperate edge to them, a kind of anxiousness to please, that turned him off. He supposed they got the job done, and that was all he really wanted to know about them.

Then he had accidentally run into Hannah on Madison Avenue about a week later. He was walking to work from Angelica's apartment after one of those horrible scenes she had treated him to at the end. Angelica dressed up was so beautiful, the soft shadows of her collarbone under her silk blouses, the golden wings of her hair, her delicate flowery perfume. But the woman he had left that morning was a skinny harridan, her skin pasted to her bones, eyes swollen with tears, and her voice hoarse from screaming accusations. You made me believe you loved me. You promised me. You lied to me. How could you? He felt tired and defeated and old as he walked past Tiffany along Fifty-seventh Street towards his office. Maybe he was too old for this. Maybe they were right. Maybe he should just get married again and have done with it.

"Hey! There's Sam Noble," Hannah had called from behind him as he turned the corner. He stopped and watched her come toward him. She certainly looked young and happy, even her walk was a lighthearted bounce.

"Hi, handsome," she said, brassy. Big grin. Was she making fun of him? "You probably don't remember me, but we met last week and I remember you."

She was so open and merry with her lit-up mischievous smile and her tously light-brown hair that it made him feel better just to stand on a street corner and watch her laugh and talk. For the first time, he noticed that it was a beautiful morning—one of those crisp New York City autumn days when the sun turns everything orange and gold, and winter is a friendly threat: just enough of a threat to make each second of warmth seem like a treasure. They were both late for work, but he asked her if she would like to have coffee anyway.

"Sure," she said. Over watery coffee at a stained Formica table in one of the greasy spoons on Fifty-sixth Street they gossiped about the boring party where he hadn't noticed her, and the new Vonnegut book, and she said she was reading Trollope, and he told her to try *The Eustace Diamonds*. She seemed to enjoy everything, even the lousy coffee. Try taking Angelica to anything less than Orsini's! And afterward, when she reached out to give his arm a friendly squeeze, and walked off down the street apparently totally unconcerned about whether she would ever see him again, he knew he would want to call her. Of course, she wasn't his type at all. A bit dowdy and definitely overweight. But there was something so hearty about her—a sense of good humor bubbling just beneath that plain surface—that he was attracted to her anyway. She made him laugh. She made him feel better. She made him feel sexy and elegant and young.

Travis was playing pretty well, he noticed, coming out of his daydream with a pleasant jolt. His jerkiness seemed to be under control and his shots were strong and well-directed.

"Keep your elbow in on those backhands," Sam suggested. "That's why your shots are going a little high." Travis actually took his advice. His backhand straightened out as he followed through. It looked good. Sam remembered his pride at Travis's starring on the St. Paul's track team. He had seemed so promising then. He was a good athlete, but his lanky body was hard to control. In tennis he had always hit the ball too hard, with a violent jerk that often sent it into the net. When that happened, he would tense up and get angry, and it would happen even more. Sam had spent days, no, weeks, no, whole summers, on tennis courts trying to get Travis to relax and play as well as he ought to. It never worked. Maybe he had been too impatient.

"Turn your side to the net! Step *forward*," he could remember yelling in the evening at the 'Sconset Casino, in the afternoon at the Dunnes' court in Bar Harbor, even on the gritty, pockmarked courts of Central Park. "Make it all one motion," he would hiss in frustration, walking across the court to demonstrate his own carefully controlled stances and swings. "Can't you make it all one motion?"

He had probably been a rotten father. He never really blew up, but Travis could certainly see that he was not pleased often enough. Who wasn't a lousy father these days, though? At least his kid wasn't on drugs or in some kind of Yoga group or walking around the streets chanting in an orange robe, with his hair shaved into a topknot, like Charley North's son. At least Travis's backhand was better and he was serving in one fluid, effective motion now. Maybe all those lessons were finally paying off. In fact, as a team, he and Travis were much too good for Hannah and Jake. She was a strong player but she needed practice. Some of her best forehands went into the net, and she played too far forward. Timing. And Jake, although he certainly deserved an A for effort, would never be more than a mediocre player. He was a real sport about it, though. His steady good humor and his ability to grin ruefully instead of getting angry when he missed an easy shot were impressive. He made Travis's wild exuberance seem a little rude.

"Six-two!" Travis called out triumphantly after the last point of the set. "We won it, Dad!"

Sam smiled at him and reached out to put a paternal hand on his shoulder. The boy was so excited Sam could almost feel the ends of his nerves vibrating under the skin. A wave of love for his son melted his guts and he felt like hugging him. He didn't, though; he didn't hug other men.

"Good set, good playing, Trav," he said. "Why don't you go over and help Jake out for a while. It's too uneven this way. Come on over here, Hannah!"

He began the second set. Standing behind the baseline, he lined the edge of his tennis sneaker up against the white tape between two of the tiny indentations where tacks held it to the clay. He tested his weight against his forward foot, mentally swinging the racket back and up through the curve of his service. He would serve a soft one to Jake's forehand, easy to return but not so easy that it would look as if he was serving that way on purpose. He didn't want to hurt Jake's feelings. God, games were complicated. He exhaled quickly as the ball went cleanly over the net to the center of the court. Good. Jake returned the ball neatly to Hannah. All right. After this set they would go back to Ballymarr and have lunch. He began to look forward to the cool, mouth-filling first beer of the day.

He changed courts and served to Travis. The serve was

low, just clearing the tape, and Travis whacked the ball into the net. Jake missed his next serve. He changed courts again and served a slow, steady ball to Travis's backhand. The boy didn't seem ready for it. He tried to run around the ball and take it as a forehand and so he missed it completely.

The next game was Travis's service. Suddenly his body looked jerky and uncoordinated. He double-faulted three times in a row.

"*Darn* it," he said, swinging angrily at the air with his racket. On his fourth serve, with the score at love-forty, he got the ball into Hannah's court. Hannah returned it hard to Jake. Jake missed it, losing the point and the game.

"Come *on*," Travis muttered. Jake didn't answer him.

Travis's game steadily deteriorated. On backhand strokes his elbow stuck out as if his arm was broken.

"Keep that elbow in," Sam reminded him from across the net. Nothing doing.

Travis's attitude made Hannah furious. No one was going to get away with picking on her kid brother. The first set was fun, she didn't care about losing. But now Travis's mood was beginning to poison the air like a thick, smothering fog. She could see that Sam was confused about his mood change. Well, she wasn't. She knew just what the matter was. If he couldn't play on Sam's side, he didn't want to play at all. What a baby. Sports were supposed to be what he was so *good* at.

His game got more erratic and violent with each point. A few times his returns to her were so hard, so loaded with anger and the intent to hurt, that she felt like ducking instead of swinging. But most of his hard shots went smacking into the net. "Stupid ball!" he would explode when this happened, or, "stupid god-damn net!" Jake got quieter and quieter. Between games, she tried to catch his eye across the net, but he was locked in some inner contemplation. Her stomach began to knot up and her forehead throbbed. She wished the game was over and they were back at Ballymarr. At least there she could retreat to her room. The sky darkened, but no rain fell.

The score was four games to one, in their favor, and Travis's serve was coming up when she turned around to collect the balls on her court. Mint new Slazengers. She bent over toward the fence to scoop one up on the rim of her racket and a ball whizzed by her right ear at top speed and smashed into the fence in front of her, sticking in the steel mesh about two feet above the clay. She turned around fast. Jake was leaning on his racket and gazing out at the moors, seemingly oblivious. Travis was standing across from him with his eyes on the ground, his racket relaxed at his side. Sam was at the edge of the court, pulling his white cable-knit sweater over his head. It was getting colder.

His head popped out of the V-neck of wool. "Come on, let's get this game going again before we all freeze to death," he said.

Serving to her, Travis double-faulted again, sending both balls into the loose mesh of the net. His first serve to Sam was a let ball, flicking the tape along the top of the net and falling into the service court. His second serve came low to Sam's forehand. Sam returned it to Travis's backhand, and Travis hit it into the net.

Serving to Hannah again, he sent the ball high and soft over the net toward her. She slanted it hard across Jake's side and won the point.

"Awwww, shit," Travis said. He hit two more serves into the net in silence. Five-one.

Hannah served to Travis now. She watched as the ball went over the net toward him and bounced in the court off the edge of the service line.

"Out, that was out!" Travis said. She certainly wasn't going to argue at this point. She served again. This time he returned the ball and she hit it back to Jake's side, a lob, high and over his head. He missed it. She changed courts to serve the ball to Jake. She was angry and hit it harder than she meant to. He returned it into the net.

"Can't you play at all?" Travis asked. Jake turned his back and stared out at the moors. He looked as if he was trying not to cry.

She'd show him. What a spoilsport! How could Sam let him pick on Jake like that? Why was he so passive? Her anger made her tense. Her throw felt off-balance and she double-faulted in quick succession. She walked across the court with her eyes down, composing herself. Her third serve to Jake was fine. She lobbed it softly over to his forehand. He returned it to Sam, who had moved up to play at the net. He angled the ball across Travis's court. Travis missed it. Forty-fifteen.

Set point. She bounced the ball twice on the ground to relax herself. Concentrate. Eye on the ball now. She threw the ball up and hit it much too soon, sending it bouncing off the court on her side of the net.

"Streeeike one," Travis said.

That little asshole. If he had been her son, she would have stopped the game right then and there and given him a severe talking to. Manners maketh man, she would have told him. And it isn't whether you win or lose. She seethed at Travis's poor sportsmanship and at Sam's failure to stop him. She threw up the second ball now and hit it straight on, her racket tilting perfectly to give it a spin from behind, her body following through.

The ball went to Travis's backhand as she had meant it to. He swung awkwardly, elbows out at an angle, legs stiff and straight, and hit it with the wooden edge of his racket. With a dull, solid sound, the ball ricocheted off the racket and popped up behind him, hitting the fence.

"Game," she said quietly, trying to moderate the satisfaction in her voice. "Game and set." There was an ominous silence. Travis stood still for a moment and they all watched him. Then, with a violent motion, he hurled his racket at the net. The loop of wood and gut crashed against one of the steel net posts and splintered. The broken racket head came to rest hanging limply from the post, the strings drooping from the shattered wood.

"Well, Frederick Culloden can certainly afford another one, that's for sure," he said. He wrenched the ruin of the racket off the post and jammed it into the garbage pail at the door of the stone hut. Sam carefully zipped his racket inside its cover and pretended not to notice. As they put the balls and rackets back in the shed in uncomfortable silence, the sky got suddenly darker and rain clouds closed in over the view from the west. It was probably already raining at Ballymarr.

Chapter

16

The knots of anxiety at the pit of her stomach dissolved
slowly with the second sip of Irish. It burned her throat and
sent a cloud of warmth and forgetfulness through her nerve
centers. The headache was gone. Rain had started to fall
now, and water streaked the leaded panes of the windows in
the anglers' bar. Travis had ordered beer instead of whiskey,
and before he had finished his glass he stood up.

"I'm going on upstairs," he said. Was he feeling chagrined
and sorry for himself? Or was he still angry and sulking?
"Why don't you come up when you're finished, Dad? I'd like
to show you a letter I got in Paris from Mom."

"Okay, kiddo," Sam said.

With Travis out of the room, they began to relax. Hannah
stretched her legs out in front of her on his vacant chair.

"Mmmmm, that feels good."

"I guess he's pretty tense about being here," Sam said. He
turned to Jake with his best man-to-man-apology manner.
We both know how tough things are sometimes. "You held
up wonderfully, Jake. Thanks."

Jake let out a long breath. It sounded as if he'd been holding it in since the middle of the tennis game.

"No problem," he said. But she knew that he was hurt. Who could blame him? Here he had left his girl and his friends in Paris only to find himself trapped in someone else's family quarrel. Worse, he was everyone's scapegoat even though he had nothing to do with the problem—or maybe *because* he had nothing to do with the problem. Jake hated trouble. He had left the miseries of his adolescence behind, but being picked on about sports reduced him to his angry, pudgy little-boy self. She would have to find a way to make it up to him.

Sam stood up now. He had finished his second Irish and he looked sleepy. "I guess I had better go and see what the matter is now," he said, rolling his eyes in a silent complaint. His silliness annoyed her and she stuck her tongue out at his receding back. Maybe that would make Jake feel better. At least she was on his side, at least she knew that all this man-to-man stuff didn't make up for what had happened on the court. Travis was impossible. But he was Sam's son. Sam shouldn't be snide about it when Travis acted badly—he should do something about it at the time. Or keep his mouth shut. If Sam didn't protect Travis, who would?

"I'm afraid that was kind of rough on you," she said to Jake.

"Don't worry about it."

"I guess Travis really is in some kind of trouble," she said.

"Looks like it." Jake stared out the window. She felt drowsy and relaxed, snuggled down in the velvety warmth of fire and whiskey. Maybe time would take care of Jake's hurt feelings. His face still looked puffy and on the verge of quivering into tears. They could go fishing and maybe he'd catch one. She searched her memory for something that Jake was very good at—preferably something that Travis was not very good at. Reading. She could hardly suggest a spelling bee. Jake turned his face toward her.

"Listen, I hope you won't be worried—I mean, it's nothing to do with today."

"What?" She saw he was blushing.

"It's just that I think I'll go back down to Paris pretty soon. I have a lot to do there."

"Oh, no!" she said, sitting straight up, surprised. "I mean, why? What's the matter? It wasn't that bad. Oh, shit, I spilled my whiskey." She rubbed frantically at the spreading wet spot on her jeans.

"Calm down, Hannah," he said. "It's no big deal. I never meant to stay more than a day or two. I just ought to be doing some work, you know, the official reason for me to be in Europe is to practice my dreadful French."

A flash of selfish irritation soured her. Jake was leaving because it was too tough for him, that was why. Why was he so passive? She would have stayed with him if their positions had been reversed.

"Are you sure it's not Helen? Are you sure you're not just afraid that she won't wait for you?"

"Don't be silly. Helen will do what she likes, regardless."

"Well, it probably won't make you seem more attractive if you go rushing right back to her, you know."

"Why don't you let me be the judge of that?"

Oh, shit. Now she had ruffled Jake's feathers too, lashing out at him because she didn't want him to go. She stared out the windows. The rain had stopped but the sky was still dark. Couldn't she get along with anybody? She reached into her sweater pocket for a cigarette. The acrid taste filled her lungs and dulled her nerves.

"How come you're smoking again? I thought you quit."

She shrugged. "Does it matter? Sam made it seem okay, I guess, and it helps me stay thin."

"Terrific logic," Jake said. "Another whiskey?" He went to the bar and came back with two neat refills. The heavy liquid sloshed as he walked, leaving a fine, translucent film against the sides of the glasses.

"Please don't be angry, Jake," she said, although she knew he would never admit to being angry. "I'm just upset about a lot of things."

"That's okay, Hannah." He reached out and touched her shoulder. "I can see you're in a bad spot. Listen, why don't you come back to Paris with me? We could have a lot of fun and leave these two guys to work it out alone for a while. It might not be a bad idea."

"No," she said before thinking. She didn't want to leave. She didn't want to go to Paris. "No, I don't think so, I might as well stay."

"Are you sure? I don't want to push you, but I feel I don't belong here and I thought you might be having some of the same feelings."

"But I *do* belong here. The whole trip and everything was my idea in the first place. Travis is only here because I nagged Sam to see him until he gave in. Travis is the outsider."

"Maybe in theory. It may have been your idea, Hannah, but it looks to me like you're the outsider now."

"But I can't accept that."

"Exactly."

"I see what you're saying, Jake, but I don't think you really understand the situation. I've talked to Sam about it and he knows how I feel." She was lying. "I just don't think I should leave right now."

"Okay, it was just a suggestion."

Jake's silence quietly urged her to reconsider. Probably it would be a good idea to go now, but she didn't want to. The thought of having to leave because Travis had chased her away from her own vacation made her contrary and stubborn. Jake was offering the perfect out. A minimum of explanation, an honorable leave-taking. She could even say she'd be back, or arrange to meet Sam and Travis later on in the trip. Sam would be a little confused, but he'd be polite about it. She just didn't want to go, that's what it came down to. She just didn't feel like leaving now that she was winning.

"I don't want to leave Sam, I guess," she said. Her voice sounded faltering and unsure.

"Well, the offer stands. You can always come later."

"When would you leave?"

"There's a four o'clock bus from Letterkenny this afternoon. I thought I could spend the night in Donegal and be back in Paris by tomorrow night."

"I didn't think it would be so soon."

"Well, if I'm going to go, I might as well go," he said. "Who knows what delightful sports events may be planned for later? I think I'll go up and start packing."

"Please don't be cross."

"Okay, why don't you come and help me pack." His voice was cool but he touched her arm as they walked upstairs. They were friends again.

She lay on Jake's bed in the narrow bedroom. His window faced away from the river and the broad stone sill obscured the view of the gravel sweep and interior lawns and gardens. Jake packed. Neatly, methodically, as if each shirt and pair of pants was a special friend, he took the clothes out of his drawers. Soft oxford shirts from Brooks, worn jeans, a green shetland sweater. Everyone she knew dressed the same way. Except Sam. The glass of fashion and the mold of form.

Jake laid the backpack on the bed at her feet and unzipped the compartments. He folded up the dirty clothes as carefully as the clean ones and tucked them in the recesses of the backpack. There were no bulges or strained seams in Jake's pack. He was almost too neat for a man. She remembered Travis's pack with its overstuffed sides and scraps of clothing caught in the zippers and the little stuffed monkey looking mournfully out of the top compartment.

Jake turned to the sink and began arranging his toothbrush, toothpaste, and shaving things in a special two-ply plastic bag that he had left an exact space for in the pack.

"I'd better go tell Sam I'm taking you to the bus station and get the car keys," she said. "I'll meet you downstairs."

"Okay." Jake was intent on precision and he didn't look up when she left.

She walked down the hall past the treacherous staircase and toward the bedroom facing the river. She was relieved to see that the door was open. Sam was there. She didn't want to have to interrupt him if he was with Travis in Travis's room. He was reading in a chair near the windows. The sky was still dark and he had switched on a reading lamp with a pale pleated shade. His thick hair gleamed. The soft light cast loving shadows on his face. What a handsome man. His legs were casually crossed to hold the book he was reading —*The Joys of Trout,* by Arnold Gingrich. How could she leave a man who looked like that? She crossed the room and sat down on the edge of his lap, perching herself on his knees and gently knocking the book over toward him so that it pressed into his stomach.

He looked up and smiled. "You're asking for it," he said.

"Just trying to get your attention."

"Have you thought of trying a tap on the shoulder, or a discreet yoo-hoo?" He let the book slide to the floor and put his arm around her. "That's what civilized people generally do to get each other's attention."

"I guess I'm not civilized, then," she said, breaking free and propping herself up on the bed with her legs crossed.

"I don't suppose there is any real reason for your wanton disruption of my scholarly activities?"

"As a matter of fact, before you distracted me I was going to ask you for the car keys."

"Where are you going, little one?" He reached into his pocket and tossed the keys onto the bed.

She looked down at the patterned bedspread between her knees. Tiny blue sprigs of forget-me-nots were framed in the angle of her jeans and boots.

"Jake decided he ought to get back to Paris and I volunteered to drive him to the bus station," she said, keeping her voice neutral and even. But Sam looked up in surprise. Damn it. She didn't want to have to explain anything.

"He's leaving already? I thought he was going to stay awhile."

"He says he's worried about his studies," she said. "He thinks he should be back there working on his French. But I think it's that he has a girl."

Sam nodded. He could understand that. "That's a shame, I certainly enjoyed having Jake with us," he said. The complacent tone of a father saying how much he had enjoyed one child's company at another child's birthday party.

"He asked me to go with him," she said. Take that, you smug old creep.

"Why on earth did he do that?" Sam said. "Doesn't he know that you're here with me?"

"Oh, I don't know." She strung it out. "I guess he just wanted company on the trip or something."

"Did you want to go?"

"Of course not, I'm here with you." She laughed.

"Well, he'll have plenty of company when he gets to Paris."

That was close. She hoped he wouldn't ask any more questions about Jake's feelings. Already she had come too near to confessing. She wanted to tell him everything and try to explain Jake, and her feelings, and ask for help. She knew he wouldn't understand, though. And even if he did, what could he do about it? There was no sending Travis away now. Even sending him home early would be out of the question. Anything she could ask him for would just make trouble. He didn't like trouble. She stood up and went behind his chair, reaching out to muss the neat waves of his hair.

"Dooon't," he whined, like a teased little boy. He grabbed her arm and pulled her around toward him. Her anger melted and she cuddled next to him, smoothing back the offending hairs and stroking his warm ears. It was easy to imagine Sam as a little boy. He had never lost the slightly petulant, very-well-cared-for air of a male child in a wealthy family. She loved him boy and man, her hugging half-sexual, half-maternal.

He nuzzled her shoulders. Contentment. Sometimes when Sam looked like a child it made her long to have a child of his—a real child who would look like that. But of course they didn't discuss it.

"I think it's time to consider this," the psychiatrist said. "You're approaching a biological deadline."

"What good is considering it going to do?"

"Perhaps you should begin to think about what you want, and how likely it is that you'll get it in terms of the men you attach yourself to."

"What do you mean?"

"I'm asking if you're being realistic about your own future."

Driving Jake to the bus station, she felt sad and exhilarated. She would miss Jake, but she was on the threshold of something interesting. Leaving with him probably would have been the sensible thing, but it was wrong to run away from difficulties and risks and painful situations. It was right to take chances. By staying, she was doing the courageous, the life-affirming thing. She was going to be magnificent.

She and Jake exchanged messages for the people they would each see first; she sent her love to friends in Paris, and he to friends in New York. Jake was very dear to her again, now that he was leaving. They rode through the green landscape to the gray streets of the town in intimate silence.

The bus was the same old red-and-white rattletrap both the boys had arrived on. As they pulled up to the bleak station platform, the driver, in a shabby black uniform and cap, was taking tickets from the last passengers. She double-parked the car and got out to settle Jake's pack on his shoulders and give him a last handshake and a kiss.

"Take care," they said to each other. What did that mean?

From the curb, she watched him disappear up the steep steps into the coach. She got back in the car and turned on the motor. Through the windows of the car and the bus she could see Jake's silhouette. He had taken a seat, and he was staring straight ahead. She waved at him, but he didn't see her. He was on his way, thinking about Donegal, and Paris after that, and forgetting about her and Travis and Bally-marr. With a roar and a belch of smoke, the bus started up and moved off slowly down the street.

The rain began as she drove back and she tried to feel dashing, alone at the wheel, down-shifting on each curve and letting the car slip sideways on the filmy wet asphalt as it gained its equilibrium. But a cloud of anxiety and loneliness blotted out the pleasure of driving. Jake was gone and she was a stranger in a strange family in a foreign land. Suddenly she was afraid of everything. She slowed down—driving so fast was dangerous. What if someone saw her speed by in this flashy car and decided to chase her? Was it safe for her to be driving, by herself, in the Irish dark?

"You know that ninety-nine, no, a hundred percent of these fears are in your head," the psychiatrist said.

"I know, but it doesn't help."

"Your fears are coming from your own memories, your own imagination."

"I try to control them. I know they don't make sense, but they don't go away."

The rain added to the darkness in the dense copse of beech and oak after the sign for Ballymarr. In the half-light the abandoned gatehouse and the rutted driveway looked even spookier than when she had first seen them. She shivered as she got out of the car to open the iron gates. Dark hands rustled the shrubbery by the side of the road. Ghosts watched her from the empty windows. Gooseflesh chilled her scalp and her heart pounded. She quickly got back in the car and slammed the door shut. Above the trees she could see the outlines of the parapets of Ballymarr. The House of Usher, the House of Noble. A setting for murder. The fumes from the moat, his dead sister, the mysteriously creaking hinge, and Roderick Usher's unearthly shriek. "She stands now without the door!"

She revved the engine up the bumpy driveway and hit the gravel with a braking turn, sending plumes of pebbles off the groomed surface. The big door stood slightly ajar. In the gloom of the hallway two men were standing close together, muttering in conspiratorial conversation.

"Hi, Travis," she said. He jumped and turned toward her. "Oh, hi."

"Sorry you didn't get to say goodbye to Jake," she said. "He left on the four o'clock bus. Hello, Conor."

"Dad told me he was gone. I guess we'll see him when we get back to New York." And he turned his back on her to take up his low-voiced conversation with the head gillie.

Chapter

17

Hannah ran up the stairs to the bedroom. She couldn't wait to see Sam. She was lonesome and frightened and he was her friend. Her beautiful friend. In spite of everything, he would comfort her. He would hold her in his arms and he would understand how much she missed Jake. When she got to the bedroom, it was empty. Across the hall in the bathroom she could hear the constant low roar of the shower and she pounded on the closed door.

"Sam, let me in," she yelled through the wooden panels. She rattled the knob but he had latched it from the inside.

"Let me in," she shouted. "I don't care if you're all wet, I need a hug." She pushed at the door impatiently; she wasn't even sure he could hear her over the noise of the water.

"I can't hear you," he called out of the shower.

"I need a hug," she shouted, raising her voice as high as she dared. "Let me in!"

"I'll be right out," he called back.

She walked across the hall and into the bedroom and curled up on the bed, withdrawing into the pillows. The hell with him, then. By the time he appeared, glowing from his shower and as pink and dry and clean as a baby, her moment of loneliness had passed.

"How come you were shouting at me when I was in the shower?" he asked. "Was there something wrong?"

"It was nothing."

She propped herself up against the flowered headboard and watched him dress. Sam didn't try clothes on and take them off and try them on again the way she did. He was deft and sure and confident. A clean blue oxford shirt, brown corduroys, and a beige cashmere sweater. Socks and shoes. No time wasted. No agonizing in front of the mirror. No desperate searching for some kind of image that will give you enough confidence just to get out the door. Mirrors were Sam's friends.

When they walked down the stairs to the dining room, Travis was waiting for them next to the rod rack in the hall.

"At last," he said. "Conor says we should definitely fish tonight. The rain has brought up the water level. And anyway, I'm starving."

They went across the room and sat down at the usual table in the angle of the windows. The table was set for four, but the waitress quickly came and took away the extra place. Travis seemed entirely recovered from his morning tantrum. He laughed and chatted as he passed the bread. He looked healthy and blood glowed through the skin of his cheeks and temples. Maybe Jake really had irritated him, maybe he just couldn't stand Jake. She could see how Jake's prudishness and his knowing so much could drive someone crazy. Especially someone like Travis, a man of action who was no good at talking. Of course she missed Jake, but it was just as well that he had left. They would all get along better now.

"You spent a lot of time with Conor this afternoon," Sam said. "Did you get any helpful information? What did you want to ask him about? Could I have the butter, please?"

"Here you go, Dad. We mostly talked about flies and stuff. He says that young German guy ties all his own, depending on the conditions each day."

"Does he think the rain is going to help us?"

"Yeah. In fact I reserved beat five for us while I was talking. It's the one you haven't fished yet. He says it's especially good when the water's high. I passed it the other day coming back from the beach and it looked terrific."

"It looks as if it's starting to rain hard again," Hannah said. "It's going to be pretty cold out there tonight." Outside, the rain was falling in gray sheets against the glassy curves of the Erninmore.

"Well, you don't have to come, then," Travis said. *"I'm* certainly going."

"I'll come."

That was the same old Travis. Touchy and angry. Was he trying to keep her from going tonight so that he could be alone with Sam? Or was he trying to taunt her into going fishing in the rain so that Sam would go, too? She didn't think he would want to be out there alone while she and Sam snuggled by the fire. She concentrated on her lamb chop. Protein would keep her warm out there tonight. The fat from the chop was already congealing in white crusts around the edge of the blue Spode dish.

Upstairs she dressed for the weather: two pairs of socks, the high rubber boots she had borrowed from the hotel's supply of fishing gear, blue jeans, a pale-blue Duofold T-shirt, her shetland sweater, and her blue slicker with the hood. She put some extra flies and leader in the pockets. She was ready, but Sam was still arranging his assortment of flies on the felt insets of his tackle jacket.

"I guess I'll go downstairs and get my rod," she said.

"Okay, see you down there. Do you think I should take this nymph just in case?"

"Sure." She walked down the stairs, moving awkwardly in

her many layers of clothing and clumping in the oversized boots. She found the rod Sam had brought for her upright in the end of the rack. A wand of delicate bamboo sections, it stretched up toward the landing. Darker brown bands punctuated the golden lacquered surface. She bent down to lift it out of its narrow slot.

"That's a grand little rod." Conor's voice made her jump. He had appeared behind her in the gloom of the hallway as she bent forward. "I hope you'll be catching something with it tonight," he said.

She looked down at the silver metal reel, clamped at the end of the rod in front of the cork grip. Generations of sweaty hands had left a worn brown stain at the center of the cork. The word ORVIS was stamped across the middle of the reel.

"I hope so, too," she said, composing herself and trying not to look as if he had scared her. "Travis says you promised us good luck on beat five."

"Yes, I did, but I didn't know it would keep up the rain this way," Conor said. "It's a real storm now. You watch your step down there, it's a dangerous piece of the river."

"How come?"

"Ah, well, now, that's where the water goes over the big weir and it's very treacherous in any storm." He drew out the words, letting the R's vibrate on his tongue. "We fished a young fellow out of there last year. He was lit up to the gills and walking in the dark. He must have slipped on those rocks and fallen in."

"Couldn't he swim?" Her heart beat with anxiety as she pictured a drowning man. Choking, coughing death.

"Ah, who knows now. I don't know how much good swimming would do you in that current. I told Travis to warn you to take extra care down there. You may have some luck with that pretty rod of yours, but watch out you don't slip."

142

She stared into Conor's blue eyes, searching for some clue of malevolence or treachery, but they were expressionless. Why hadn't Travis warned her, then? Conor turned away from her and walked off down the hall to the anglers' bar.

She would take care, all right. Would she ever; would she ever! She imagined Travis, like Iago, laying his secret plans. A tragic incident in a remote Irish river. The circumstances were different, but it was the same old green-eyed monster —jealousy. *We were never sure exactly how it happened. But by the time we got to her it was too late. No, Jake had left that very day. . . .*

No, she was being silly. Nightmares and fantasies were forming in the half-light of the hallway. These things don't really happen. The psychiatrist had said her fears were imaginary. And when Travis bounded down the stairs in his slicker and sneakers he looked like a friendly puppy-dog of an American boy, not a twisted plotter against innocent lives. She was stupid and melodramatic. He was just a kid, a sad, absentminded, mixed-up kid.

"Hi, Travis," she said, trying to catch his eye for reassurance.

He avoided her gaze and bent over to get a rod out of the rack. "Hi," he mumbled down toward his sneakers. "Where's Dad?"

Sam appeared at the top landing in full fig. He always dressed for everything, and now he looked like a model for the fishing department of Orvis or Abercrombie or L. L. Bean or all three. His soft corduroys were tucked smoothly into high boots with rubber soles, and he wore an old dark-green turtleneck under his blue cabled shetland. A red bandanna was knotted around his throat. Somehow he looked foppish and sportsmanlike at the same time. Under his slicker she caught a glimpse of the tackle jacket with its rows of neatly arranged flies.

"If I were a trout, I'd be stunned by your elegance," she said as he clumped down the stairs toward them.

"Let's hope so. Let's hope that you would want to get caught by me."

"I always feel like getting caught by you," she said. Sam gave her shoulder a pat, Travis looked up from the rack, and they started out through the courtyard and down the hill in the rain.

She could hear the fat, soft raindrops falling on the ground around them as they walked, and see the dappled pattern of them on the water. The earth smelled of pine and heather. As they got closer to the lough the water boiled up into rapids in the rain-swollen river. At the second weir, the sound of it rushing over the weir wall drowned out the pattering of the rain. They passed the wooden post which marked the beginning of beat five. Sam stopped and signaled over the noise that he was going to stay there and fish from the rocks above the big third weir. Below them, at the bottom of a furze-covered bank, a crumbling stone pier jutted out into the water and Hannah started down to it. Travis pointed farther downstream and disappeared through the laurel and gorse bushes in the direction of the lough.

There was still light in the sky, but through the rain the air had the ominous feeling of an approaching thunderstorm. As she stood alone at the end of the pier cold bit through her layers of clothing. The wind screeched in the trees behind her. She craned her neck to see if she could get a glimpse of Sam, but the rocks where he stood were hidden by a curve in the shoreline. She longed for romance, for a man to sweep her off into the mystery of the storm with his passion. *Wild nights, wild nights / Were I with thee, / Wild nights should be / Our luxury.* Did Emily Dickinson fish for trout in the streams around Amherst? Did she rush out of her father's house in the stormy nights, letting the wind tear at her crown of braided hair? Was she afraid?

From the protection of her slicker hood, Hannah could see the rain lashing at the black water that raced by the pier where she stood. She had had to pick her way out carefully over the uneven stones, but it was a perfect place to cast from. On the other side of the whirlpool below the weir, upstream, water seethed against a rock wall shadowed by giant oaks that leaned over to drag their lowest leaves in the river. Farther downstream a breakwater of stones threw the water foaming into the air.

She cast from the end of the pier straight across the pool toward the trees, planting her feet carefully on the treacherous mossy surface before pulling in the line. Her oversized boots made her feel clumsy and badly balanced. Pull, cast, reel it in. Water slid down the shiny arms of the jacket, and she could hear rain beating on the surface of her hood. But none of the rain had penetrated the warm enclosure of underwear, sweaters, and socks next to her skin.

Pull, cast, reel it in. The shining waves of black in the whirlpool took on strange shapes; a bubbling oil slick, a great pile of onyx boulders, the billowing skirts of Eustacia Vye, drowned for love in the weir at the edge of Egdon Heath.

Pull, cast, reel it in. There was a nibble! Or perhaps it was just a sharp eddy in the pulls of the current. She reeled in quickly and cast again, too clumsily. The fly slapped down upstream and the white of the oiled silk line bunched up in a tangle on the water. Another cast. There, she felt it again. A definite tug this time, he was coming up from the depths to her fly. She pictured the fish, trying to gauge the moment when the fly would be deep enough in his bony mouth so that she could jerk the rod up and set the hook. But when she pulled the rod up in a short, abrupt motion, the line was empty again. The noises and distractions of the storm faded as she imagined him just out of reach below the surface of the water. Elusive silver swimmer. But after two more casts across the pool, the line stayed slack, the fly uninterrupted as she played it across the water.

Rain splashed harder against her hood now, and one cold drop made a chilling progress down her neck and spine. The trees across the water were going out of focus in the fading light, turning to massive Druid shapes above the river. In the darkness, the face of the drowned boy floated in the pool below her. *Fear death by water.* She began to worry about getting back down the long slippery pier. Pulling in her rod, she turned to assess the distance back to the shore. Travis was standing right behind her. His slicker was tied up tightly around his face so that she could hardly see his features as she looked up at him. In the shadows she seemed to see the stony, malevolent expression that had been on his face after the tennis game. Cringing, she took a step back away from him down the pier. Her heart pounded and an icy sweat formed under the rubbery jacket. Travis leaned down and touched her arm with his hand.

"Hey, are you all right?" he said.

She nodded numbly.

"I came to ask if you've got any extra leader. I lost mine on a snag down there." She could see his face now. His eyes looked gentle and confused. His hand felt warm and steady against her sleeve.

"You look kind of cold," he said. "Do you want a hand back to the bank?"

"No, I'm okay. Really."

"No leader, though?"

"No, no leader." Travis shrugged and turned his back. His long legs carried him down the long pier and into the darkness and underbrush in a moment. She peered after him, half wishing she had asked for help getting back to the bank, but he was gone. Squinting through the rain, she saw the beam of Sam's flashlight bobbing back and forth from farther up the bank in the other direction as he walked toward her. When he got to the base of the pier, the light swung in erratic arcs as he crashed through the bushes. Keeping his light off the water, he picked his way out toward her.

"Don't you feel like going in?" he asked, raising his voice above the wind. "It's raining harder and it's getting late."

"Sure, let's go in." The light evaporated her anxiety.

"Have you seen Travis?"

"I think he's farther down."

"Well, I suppose he'll come in when he's ready to."

She pushed the hook of her fly into the cork and reeled the line in tight against it.

"Let's go, then." Sam led the way with the flashlight, stepping carefully to avoid the slippery moss, and pulling the bushes open for her when they got to the base of the pier. The castle loomed above them, casting a pattern of reflected lights on the water below it. As they crossed the gravel in the rain she could see through the front window. A lamp with a flowered shade threw velvety shadows on the warm interior.

Soon they were stripping off their wet slickers and sweaters in the anglers' bar in front of the big fire. The wet wool steamed and gave off a musty smell as it dried on the fire screen. Peat crackled and a glass of whiskey cozied her as she sank into a safe chair. Sam stood in front of the fire, fussing with the drying clothes.

"Well, I guess your son is the only one of us who has the grit to stay out there on a night like this," Conor said. "It's quite a storm that blew up out there."

"Yes, I guess so," Sam said. He laughed. He sounded proud of Travis's stubbornness.

"Pretty rough out."

"When Travis decides to do something, it's not easy to get him to give up." Sam took a sip of his whiskey and sat down in the chair next to her. Conor stood. She could see that he would have liked to sit down, too, but some unspoken law forbade it unless Sam invited him to. "He'll come in when he's good and ready," Sam said. "Probably with a fish —or a nice case of double pneumonia."

Conor wandered across the room toward another seated couple, to stand and talk a minute with them. She sat back, letting herself relax at last. Now she wanted to see Travis. She wanted to scrutinize his expression from the safety of her chair. Why didn't he come in? How long could he stay out there in that storm? She willed him to appear in the doorway. She imagined his soft tread in the hall.

She ordered another whiskey and dawdled over it, trying to keep up a conversation with Sam. The other seated couple left and Conor got up and turned out the lights around the wooden bar. Her eyelids felt weighted down and she struggled to look alert. Where was he?

"Let's go on up, sweetie, I'm beat," Sam finally said. She had finished her drink and there were no more excuses. "It's bedtime."

She felt like a sleepy child being hustled up to bed before the excitement of the evening was over. *In summer quite the other way / I have to go to bed by day.* But she couldn't think of a reason that Sam would accept not to go. On the way up the stairs she noticed the time on the face of the grandfather clock at the landing. It was just midnight.

Chapter

18

Hannah had fallen asleep quickly, but now she was awake again. She danced the horizontal choreography of insomnia: right side, back, left side, stomach, curled up, stretched out. But her eyes stayed open, her mind alert. She shut her eyes and visualized a split-rail fence and a crowd of sheep jockeying for position behind it. One of them cantered up to it and jumped over to her side. Another one followed. Three. Four. Sam snored loudly in his sleep and she stopped counting.

He lay with his back to her, breathing heavily and occasionally rasping his breath through his throat, or his nose, or wherever snores come from. One, she chanted silently. One, one, one. She concentrated her whole self on the mantra, blocking all other thoughts from her mind. One, one, one.

Her eyes popped open again. Was that a noise outside the room in the hall? The leather traveling clock that Sam had bought at the Geneva airport ticked on the bedside table, its phosphorescent second hand sweeping along in time. Five fifteen. Who would be up at this hour? Then she heard another noise, the creak of a board as someone stealthily passed their doorway. Had they stopped? She sensed a presence, a darkness within the darkness on the other side of the door, and she waited, holding her breath. Wasn't that the quiet, careful *click, click, click* of the doorknob being tried from the outside? The door was locked but she lay frozen still between the sheets now, her heart beating with tiny thumps against her rib cage. Footsteps receded in the corridor. Sam sighed in his sleep. She strained for more warnings of nighttime danger. Silence. Below the windows she could hear the rush of the water.

"I'm so afraid of the dark," she told the psychiatrist. "I have to get up at night and check the other room in my apartment all the time."

"What are you afraid of finding? What is it that you imagine?" the psychiatrist asked.

"I don't know, I'm just afraid," she laughed. "I don't want to die."

Death could come in so many ways. A knock at the door in the afternoon, the screeching of tires behind you, a noise in the next room that at first seemed to be the wind. It could start with a cough, or an odd-looking mole on the skin, or a tiny lump somewhere just under the surface of the flesh. Or it could come from above, falling through the air, or in an airplane. The door rattling loose, a bolt stripping its threads as the plane passed over Greenland. The worst fear she had was of a death at the hands of another person. Someone she couldn't reason with or control. A man.

At home in New York she would wake up at night in a sweat of terror. Her heart would be pounding and her eyes focused on an imaginary intruder just outside the window or beyond the bedroom door. She would turn on all the lights and sit for a while in the living room to calm herself. There was no one there. But she imagined a hooded figure waiting for her with an expectant leer. Crouching behind the door in the shadows of the hallway or the lobby. A man wearing gloves—black gloves, and a ski mask to cover his face. A man in a stocking mask, horribly distorted by the suggestive surface of the nylon pressed against his features. A man who had come for her. Was Travis, or another man, out there now, trying their door, wandering the halls malevolently? Lying there helpless, she remembered how close they were to the border with Northern Ireland, and she thought about the Provos, murderous terrorists with determined, angry faces. Maybe they used the Ballymarr woods as a hiding place. She began to wonder if they were safe here at all.

She curled her body close to Sam's for protection. He had faced danger, he had fought in a war and defeated death. The shapes of the wing chairs and the big wardrobe against the wall grew distinct in the pale dawn. Her fears always evaporated in the daylight. Of course nothing would happen here, to her. Here.

She got out of bed and went to the windows. The rain had stopped and the air was clear and quiet except for the murmur of the Erninmore. A sunrise oozed hot and rosy over the lough from the east. The chirpy beginnings of birdsong began and above the hills the sky turned deep-pink like the inside of a ripe melon on a summer day. Was Travis up, too, standing at the window of his room down the hall? Watching the sunrise? And thinking about her?

She turned back to the bed where Sam slept. His blue Brooks Brothers pajamas with the darker-blue piping hung neatly over the chair next to the bed. The chambermaid had probably laid them there. Chambermaids hated sex; they always knocked on the door, or even unlocked it and poked their heads in, just at the wrong moment. "Housekeeping," they would sing out gleefully, or "Maid service," mingling with the moans and grunts of the last delicious moments of it. Her memory of sex in hotels was scored with the sounds of unlatching doors and the maids' voices and the man saying, "Oh, damn it!"

She had finally teased Sam about his pajamas so much that he had stopped wearing them. He didn't even unpack them, at least when he was with her. But he still brought them along. Security pajamas. Curled up with his arms hugging the pillow, he looked more than ever like a little boy. The white bumps of the war scars on his shoulder were completely incongruous—more like the scrapes from a playground injury or a bad fall off the jungle gym while Nanny wasn't paying attention.

Sam didn't have any trouble sleeping. He breathed in and out with serene regularity as she stared at him. The sleep of a little boy. The sleep of the just. The sleep of the innocent, the out-of-it, the oblivious, the totally self-absorbed. Had Sam ever seen sunrises, or listened to the first gentle chirping of the morning birds? It was hard to imagine him wandering around with nothing but his own fears for company. Sam didn't have night fears. Or else he didn't express them. His veneer was so perfect it was hard to tell which. He never cried, but did he even ever feel like crying any more? It was hard to picture Sam crying, or shouting, or really breaking down at all. He must have suppressed these reactions so long ago that he didn't have them any more. It was all ancient history, set in stone before she even met him.

No, Sam never would have been afraid like this. He wouldn't even have been awake. If he was worried, he would have done something or gone out somewhere. New York was full of ways to avoid facing the dark if you wanted to, especially for a man like Sam. The ballet. Elaine's. Bobby Short's second show at the Carlyle. He would have arranged something to pass the time. He would have had a plan.

Chapter

19

She leaned in close to the mirror over the sink. A network of red threads surrounded the dark-brown center of her eye. Underneath it the skin was laced with fine wrinkles, and a tracery of blue veins cast their color outward from somewhere deep under the surface. Her eyelids were puffed out below the brow bone in a puckery shelf. A tiny muscle jerked involuntarily somewhere beneath the left one, and deeper lines framed her mouth and cut across her forehead.

She had been very unhappy about the way she looked when she was young. Too fat, she had thought, or hair too curly. How blithely, how stupidly she had counted on the quality of young skin! Its lustrous smoothness under a tan, the firmness of thighs and shoulders; its air of fitting the body perfectly, with no slack or tightness. Now she was older. Too old, anyway, to stay up most of the night without showing it. Her tongue felt like leather, her head was stuffed with cotton. Mechanically, she pulled on her jeans and a sweater. Sam had already gone down to breakfast and she didn't particularly want to face him. His relentless perfection was infuriating when she felt lousy, but she did want some coffee. Maybe coffee would help.

She walked down the stairs toward the dining room. There was no chance of her falling again, in the daylight, but she walked next to the banister anyway. The sun, strained through the colors of the stained-glass window on the landing, threw golden patterns on the carpet. It was a beautiful day. No doubt Sam would have planned some little trip or outing by the time she got downstairs. She didn't want to go anywhere. She would plead a headache; it was odd how men were always willing to believe women had headaches. She would say she felt bad and get out of it, whatever it was. Instead, she would lie in the sun.

"Coffee, please," she said, making a joke of her tiredness and lifting a limp hand to her head as she sat down. Under her gesture, she examined Travis. If he had been up all night, he certainly wasn't showing the strain. His skin was smooth and color flushed across his cheekbones just under the skin. His eyes sparkled. No wrinkles, no black shadows, no deep creases in the flesh the way Sam had around his eyes and mouth. His teeth flashed straight and white as he bit into a piece of toast from the silver rack on the table. American upper-middle-class milk-drinker's teeth. The way he concentrated on his own pleasure gave him the unself-conscious grace of an animal—a cat, preening alone in the sun. She watched him carefully. He will never be this beautiful again, she thought with a mixture of admiration and satisfaction. This is his moment. Age will take the glow from his skin and unbalance his lanky symmetry. Worry will cloud his grace, speed up his pulse rate, make him fat.

"How late did you stay out?" his father asked.

"Not too long after you came in. When I came back, Conor was still up. He said you had just retired," Travis mimicked Conor's brogue unsuccessfully. "I guess the only thing you could catch out there last night was a cold."

"I don't think that's a good beat for bad weather, anyway," Sam said. "The fish are there and the water's so roiled up they can't see you. But the wind is bad and those rocks are pretty treacherous at night."

She looked sideways at Travis. His face was serene and unfathomable.

"Conor told me the currents in that whirlpool could drown someone," she said, focusing on his eyes.

"Oh, I don't think they would hurt a good swimmer," he said. "The guy that drowned down there probably panicked and got sucked into the current. Conor said he was stoned. Anyway, I get the impression the Irish don't swim very well." His tone implied that a strong crawl was a mark of racial superiority.

"A guy drowned down there?" she asked, faking surprise.

"Yeah. Didn't Conor tell you about that? He warned me that that beat was kind of dangerous and I told him to tell you and Dad about it. Didn't he?"

"Oh, well, I think he kind of mentioned it . . . would you like some of this bacon?" She changed the subject, smartingly aware that she had been trapped in a lie. Sam or Travis could find out in a minute that Conor *had* told her about the drowned boy.

After breakfast she wandered out on the terrace with a book. Getting away from Sam hadn't been hard after all; in fact he and Travis had gone upstairs together without even noticing her. She hugged the book against her side. On a trip, Sam always planned his reading to include books about the places he was going or the things he was going to do. She was the opposite. She only brought a book if she was in the middle of it. Usually she just read whatever she found in hotel bookshelves or local shops. The possibility of a discovery far outweighed the occasional risk of having to read a boring book or even having nothing to read at all sometimes. She remembered with a vivid, self-congratulatory thrill how she had happened on *Daniel Deronda* in the bookcase at The Bear at Oxford, and the afternoon it was too icy to ski, which she had spent reading Parker Perry's copy of Nabokov's *Speak, Memory*, curled up in a chair at the Green Mountain Inn. At Ballymarr she had found an old red cloth-bound set of Thomas Hardy. She had never read *Tess*, and she set to it now with relish. The bleakness of the Wessex landscape and the primitive country people seemed appropriate to the empty Irish bogs and this strange ancient Gaelic race. From the beginning, when she opened the book to the women's May Day dance, she relaxed. She was in good hands.

She sat down on a low stone seat and turned to the postcard she was using as a bookmark. Tess was speaking, finally, with Angel Clare. Although Hannah knew better—she had read other Hardy novels—she began to hope for the best. Tess was walking down toward the river with Angel when Travis appeared from around the corner. Without speaking, he sat down on the stone bench next to hers, stretching his long legs over the flagstones in the sun.

"I'm probably interrupting you," he said.

She looked up. "No, that's okay. Where's Sam?"

Travis frowned. "He's up with Conor learning to tie flies."

"You didn't want to learn?"

"Conor says he'll teach me later. It's easier with just one person." He sounded angry.

"You can't be with your father *all* the time," she said cheerfully.

"Maybe not, but I don't need some *gillie* taking up his time and telling me to get lost." She could imagine him saying *woman* instead of *gillie* in the same disgusted tone of voice.

"Maybe he wants to learn by himself."

"I doubt it." Travis sounded confident that Sam shared his desire for them to be always together.

"He needs time to himself, and he needs time with me too," she said.

156

"Well, if he didn't want to see me, why the hell did he drag me halfway across the world to be with him?" Travis challenged her.

"He did want to see you, but that doesn't mean he wants to be with you every minute. Of course he wanted to see you." Maybe she could defuse some of Travis's anger. Now he arched his back with his hands behind his head and faced up toward the sun.

"And he always gets what he wants," he said. "Mr. Perfect."

"Is that what you think?"

"Sure. The whole time I was growing up, that was all I heard about. How lucky I was to have a father like Sam. He could play tennis better than anyone else's dad, and sail better, and even publish books better. It seemed as if he could do anything."

"That must have been nice."

"Nice? It was as if he was God or something."

"Did you think he was?"

Travis looked out toward the river and leaned forward on his knees. He was lankier than Sam, but she noticed the neatness of the bones in his tanned ankles and wrists. The sun played color tricks with the glossy surface of his hair. "I don't know," he said.

"Usually people stop thinking of their parents as God by the time they reach adolescence."

"I know he's not God, for Christ's sake." Her preachy tone had released his anger, his voice hissed like steam coming out of a radiator valve. "I know that. Look at the way he treated my mother. Look at the way he let me walk out of his life. Look at the way all he cares about is his own self-improvement programs. I know he's not God. Sometimes I wonder if he's even human."

His indignation silenced her. They sat in the sun. Doubled

157

over on the bench, Travis's body looked lean and firm and coiled for a spring. The river gurgled below them.

"What are you reading?" he said finally.

"Oh, *Tess,* you know, Hardy's *Tess.*"

"Sure," he said sarcastically.

Of course he didn't know. "Sorry, it's *Tess of the D'Urbervilles* by an English novelist named Thomas Hardy. Didn't you read any Hardy in school? *The Mayor of Casterbridge,* or *Far from the Madding Crowd?*"

"I'm a lousy reader," he said. He made it sound as if this was someone else's fault.

"What about at school?"

"I avoided it."

"Didn't your teachers notice it? Didn't they try to help you?"

"Oh, sure, I was in every stupid remedial reading class in every stupid school I ever went to. Big deal."

"Maybe you had some kind of reading disability."

"Yeah, I just couldn't do it."

Before she had met Travis, she remembered, she had worried that he hadn't gotten enough attention. It was a lot easier to talk to him when Sam wasn't around.

Behind them, the comforting clink of china and silver came from the dining room, where the tables were being set for lunch. She was hungry. She reached for the pack of cigarettes she had put beside her on the stones and tapped one out of its cellophane package. Travis watched from his bench without offering a light as she fished around in her pockets for a match. Smoke filled her lungs and the back of her throat and dulled the pangs stirring in her stomach.

"I bet you didn't always smoke," he said, back to his old belligerent tone.

"I did in college, but then I quit."

"What made you start again?"

"I don't know."

"Was it when you met Dad?"

"I guess so."

"You shouldn't, you know. It's so bad for you. It's a disgusting habit." He shook his head.

"I know, I know."

"It gives you cancer and wrinkles and messes up your whole system." He sounded so confident that she felt like a child.

"I said I know."

Travis wasn't one to take a hint, though. "If you know, why do you do it?"

Hannah stubbed the cigarette out on the stones. Her pleasure was gone. The grainy brown tobacco split the fragile paper under her fingers.

"Let's go have lunch," she said.

Sam was already in the dining room, sitting at their table, reading through his half-glasses. A professor of literature, traveling alone.

"Come on, Dad, put away your book, we're famished." Travis sat down and scooped up the breadbasket.

"Bread?" He passed the basket, filled with its warm bundle wrapped in soft linen. The bread in Ireland in general, and the bread at Ballymarr in particular, was unusually good. Crusty soda bread, fresh and cakey and served with thick, sweet butter. She leaned across Sam to get a piece for herself.

"What are you reading?" she asked to distract attention from her boardinghouse reach. She broke the biscuit-colored crust, releasing a fragrant cloud of steam, and pressed a slab of butter against it with her knife as she savored her hunger.

"You shouldn't fill up on bread," Sam said.

"Is that the title of the book?" When she felt hurt or pushed away, she often passed it off with a joke. Everybody loves a clown. Who was Sam to tell her not to fill up on bread, anyway? She took a big bite but it tasted dry and sawdusty. Her hunger was gone.

"Are we going fishing again this afternoon?" Travis asked. "I guess between us we've covered every beat on this river."

"It's pretty limited," Sam said. "Too bad we can't go over and fish at Frederick's."

"Why can't we?"

"He's still away and they don't let anyone just wander around there the way you would if you were fishing. I had to get special permission to use the tennis court, in fact."

"How come?" Travis asked.

"His property is right on the border with Northern Ireland. It's very carefully regulated. I was talking to him and he says he has a small army of guards for the place."

"Hey, that's exciting!" Travis looked really interested now.

"You wouldn't think it was so exciting if you knew more about it," Sam said. "It's more awful than exciting." There was something in his voice that reminded Travis that he was young and a highschool dropout. Just as there had been something before that had reminded Hannah that, by his standards at least, she was overweight. Sam would never actually say anything like that, of course. He was too polite.

"Well, it is sort of exciting to be close to a real war zone," she said. "The war is a big part of what's happening in Ireland now. We even saw a few unpleasant things on our way up here."

"Really? Like what?" Travis asked.

"Oh, just a couple of roadblocks," she said. "No big deal."

Chapter

20

The subject of Northern Ireland percolated in Hannah's mind. Obviously it would be ridiculous to go over there— wars aren't tourist attractions. But it was so close. She had seen so many pictures and television clips of the war in Ireland that it seemed more Irish than the abandoned green landscapes and fallen-down castles of the counties they had driven through. The barbed wire and the desperate graffiti of Belfast were as familiar to her as the starving children in Cambodia or the Afghan rebels skulking in their caves.

She had taken the privilege of wealthy isolation for granted. When people like Sam came to Ireland, they came to visit the beautiful Ireland, the literary Ireland, and to take advantage of the low prices in a depressed country. They counted on Irish friendship and the island's boozy congeniality—blocking out the other side of the passionate character, which kept the country locked in a civil war. A few miles east of them there was another Ireland, a world away from the placid rhythms and rich people's country life at Ballymarr. There was an Ireland of terror and night murders and gangs who would rape you or kill you or worse if you went out with a Catholic . . . or with a Protestant. That was the real Ireland, not this shimmering dream of a country where people complained about the cooking.

In the afternoon she stood on the shore above a little stone bridge. Sam and Travis were somewhere below her on beat two.

"I'll fish with you, Dad," Travis had said as they left the castle. "You can show me what you learned about the flies."

Alone again, she squinted in the sunlight, so bright that she could see every weed and plant waving slowly at the bottom of the river. Had she come all this way to be alone, casting and recasting on the banks of a foreign river? Her heart wasn't in it. Looking up, she saw the castle, framed by green hillsides, more than ever like a mirage in a fairy tale. But the specter of Northern Ireland made the beauty of Ballymarr seem unreal and superficial. She was somehow removed from the loveliness of the scene around her, as if she was watching herself from a great distance.

At dinner Travis was bubbling with confidence. He had caught three trout, and even Conor congratulated him.

"Well, folks, I guess I'm pretty good at this fishing business," he bragged.

Sam beamed. "Maybe we can have the kitchen fry them up for breakfast," he said. "There's nothing like fresh trout."

"Was that fresh trout we had at Culloden's?" The appetizer of *Truite en Gelée* had been so elaborately trimmed that it looked like a pastry. "It was so dressed up that it was hard to tell."

"It was fresh, but he keeps his own trout pond for the kitchen. The chef's assistant just pulls out whatever he needs with a net the way they do in France," Sam said. "It's too bad that they have to be so careful about who fishes there. It's a shame that a bunch of idiot revolutionaries end up controlling something like that." He sounded as if the loss to sportsmen sustained because of the war in Northern Ireland was a personal affront.

"What makes you say they're such idiots?" Travis asked. "I don't understand what's so bad about Ireland for the Irish. It is their country, isn't it?"

"I'm afraid it's more complicated than that, Travis. War is more than just the good guys against the bad guys. The British are here as a peacekeeping force."

"They don't seem to be doing a very good job," she said.

"Don't you see how you're oversimplifying the situation? You should inform yourself a little before you draw any conclusions. If the British weren't here, it would be worse. The Protestants and the Catholics would massacre each other."

"Did they do that before the British arrived?" Travis asked.

"That's an absurd question. The British have been here off and on for centuries. I know everything looks black-and-white when you're young, Travis, but this is an ancient, tangled struggle. If you don't understand it, you shouldn't talk about it."

"Thanks for the vote of confidence, Dad." Sam's scorn had evaporated Travis's pleasure in his fishing triumph. Now he looked angry and confused.

Sam pushed back his dinner plate. "Listen, Travis, you can just thank God that you don't know what war is like. You've never seen one and I pray that you never will." His voice reverberated with the authority of his own experience.

"Why don't we drive over and have a look, then?" Travis was taunting his father now. "Maybe that will help me to be less simpleminded." His sarcasm surprised her; Sam's condescending manner had released some secret spring of bitterness in his son's mind.

"You won't like what you see," Sam said.

"At least I will have seen it."

"I'm not afraid to drive you over there, Travis," Sam said. "I'm just afraid that you'll be horrified, and sorry too."

"I should say that would be for me to decide." Travis got up and walked out of the dining room.

"You sure came down hard enough on him," she said.

"Oh, Christ!"

Hannah had never seen Sam so angry. "He just doesn't know what he's talking about. If he had ever been anywhere near a real war, he wouldn't be so dense." The bitterness was mutual.

"Well, he certainly isn't going to learn anything from you." Suddenly she began to understand how Travis's academic problems had gotten so serious. When he failed, Sam got irritated instead of trying to help.

"Okay, okay." He slapped his hand down hard on the table. "I was too hard on him, I've always been too hard on him. You don't have to make me feel any worse about it than I already do."

"Maybe if you talked about it, you might understand your reactions better. Maybe you could break your pattern of anger," she said. "Have you ever thought about going to a therapist?"

Sam put his head in his hands now. "I just don't understand," he moaned. "Why on earth would anyone want to see something awful and heartbreaking if they don't have to? It would just ruin our trip, that's all."

"Well, it does seem a little hypocritical to come to Ireland and just see the beautiful part."

"Why the hell not! We're on vacation. We didn't come here to see a war, we came to rest and relax."

"But it's so close."

"That doesn't mean we have to get involved with it. We

are here as tourists. We've come to a *grand luxe* hotel which happens to be in the North of Ireland; we help the country by bringing in dollars. They're glad to have us."

Sam pushed his chair away from the table, signaling the end of the conversation. She followed him into the library. Ignoring her, he sat down at the desk and took out a sheet of writing paper and his pen. He didn't want to talk about it any more.

She sat down behind him and stretched out her legs. Now that they had all gotten into a fight about it, she couldn't help being a little bit on Travis's side. Sam was so patronizing. Why did he have to make everything he had done that they hadn't done sound like such a big deal? Northern Ireland couldn't be *that* bad. They should just go over and have a look. In her opinion, Sam owed it to Travis to try to educate him instead of criticizing him for his curiosity. Danger and passion beckoned her. She let Sam finish writing his letter.

When he had sealed it and was pressing the green Irish stamp on, she got up and went over to him. She put her hand on his shoulder and kissed his temple.

"Wouldn't you like some coffee or a drink?" she asked.

"That would be great—let's have some coffee." He went down the hall to order it, and she sat back. Patience. She poured his coffee and waited until he had started to drink it.

"You know," she said, as if she were just thinking out loud between sips, "we could just cross the border into Northern Ireland for a few hours. It would show Travis that you do take him seriously, and it might be interesting."

He leaned back and took a deep breath. She had calculated well; he wasn't going to fight any more. "All right," he said in the tone of a parent who is finally badgered into giving in to his children's demands. Later they will find out he was right. "All right. If you and Travis want to go that much,

I'll see what I can do. Maybe there's something over there to see besides the barracks and bunkers you two have set your heart on. I think I remember hearing that Londonderry is a lovely city."

"The City of Londonderry was built in the early years of plantation by Scottish and German and English Protestants who had been induced to settle in Catholic Ireland through large land grants given by the Crown," he read aloud in a didactic singsong later that evening. They sat attentive, like eager students, in the library. *"The city of Derry itself was given over by the Crown to the citizens of London, many of whom came to settle in Ireland and who renamed the city Londonderry. A charming settlement on a hill above the River Foyle, Londonderry is principally built of red brick with spacious bay windows and dormered roofs. Constructed around a graceful square known as the Diamond, it has a lovely Tudor Gothic Guildhall and one of the largest Protestant churches in the North. The entire city is enclosed by a great town wall with crenelated towers and a promenade atop the wall on which pedestrians can stroll from Waterquay to Bishopsgate and enjoy the views the river and landscape afford."*

"Sounds nice," Hannah said. More and more, crossing the border seemed like a good idea. It would be fun to see a city with its crowds and shops and museums. Maybe there would be wonderful things to buy. Londonderry was probably so close to the border that life was almost normal there, not like the horrors of Belfast. They would walk around the promenade atop the great wall with the city and the landscape spread out before them.

Sam took a map from under the leaves of the well-worn guidebook and spread it out on the table. Shifting from his teaching manner to his planning manner, he pointed out the route he had already marked in blue pencil. Any trip worth taking is worth taking well. She peered around his shoulder at the gray block of squares labeled *Derry* at the lower right-hand corner of the map. It looked as if they would have wonderful views of both Lough Foyle and Lough Swilly from the wall. Maybe there would be a little cafe built into the ramparts of the city, like the Chèvre D'Or at Éze-Village, perched high out above the Mediterranean. They would drink wine and have lunch and spend a wonderful sunny afternoon there.

"We'll drive down beyond Letterkenny to Pluck and then up this way past Dooish Mountain to Newtown Cunningham," Sam said. She followed his pencil along one of the roads on the zigzag network of green, red, and brown lines across the map. Ireland was pale-green with brown for mountains and hills and cliffs. It looked like a lawn after a very rough winter.

"There's an important ruined castle up there on Greenan Hill." Sam pointed to a pale-brown spot between Ardnamoyle and Manner's Town. *Grianan Aileach,* a stone fort.

"The fort was built in the seventh century as a summer home for the O'Neill chieftains," Sam said. "I read somewhere that it's been ruined by overzealous reconstruction, but we'll see. Then we can cross the border above Derry and spend the rest of the morning there. I'd like to see the guildhall and the church. After that we'll drive down through Ballymagorry and have lunch at Strabane. See it on the map?"

He pointed to a cluster of streets at the very end of the wide part of the River Foyle, where the millimeter of white depicting the water on the map turned to a thread of blue.

"There's a cafe on the river there that Frederick Culloden mentioned to me," he said. "According to him it's a pretty rough place, but they have this terrific lamb stew. Trust him to find the gourmet cooking in a war zone." He paused for an indulgent chuckle. "Then we can drive back out and be home by early afternoon." On the map, the border made a livid red line across the soft patches of green and brown.

Chapter

21

They got up early and cooked breakfast in the Ballymarr kitchens. Sam was at his best, glowing with health and being in charge. He showed them how to clean the trout in a sink the size of a wading pool. He made fresh coffee and toast for three in a toaster for a dozen pieces. Sweet butter oozed into the rough brown surface of the toasted bread.

"Best meal I've had since we got here," she said. The coffee was strong and delicious. Its fumes cleared her head. And they were all in good spirits. Travis had gotten his way. Hannah had coaxed Sam into something with her cajolery and her suggestions. Sam was the leader. After breakfast he stacked their dishes in the sink. The bones of the filleted trout lay naked across the blue-and-white Spode.

"Okay, let's go," he said. Travis folded into the back of the car and she and Sam got in front. The air was cool but balmy. It ruffled her hair and clothing as they followed the road around the bottom of Lough Swilly and northward in the early morning. It was a crisp summer day, a day for women in flowered dresses, and croquet on velvety lawns, and men in tennis whites drinking highballs with mint sprigs on terraces under striped awnings after the game.

Were people who lived that way aware of how they looked from the outside? Did they know that the way they dressed and talked and even stood—casually leaning against a column or a polo pony—was the substance of fantasy for most people? Oh, of course they knew. No one was innocent. It was just a measure of their breeding that they pretended not to.

For they are the authors of dreams. Men and women whose imitators appear in advertisements for things with names like Chivas Regal and Polo and Porsche. They create the life that poor kids imagine as they lie awake in furnished rooms off Flatbush Avenue or South Main Street. And in the end those boys, after they become doctors and businessmen, in the end they have to have the same things. Boats and racehorses and croquet sets and houses with preposterous lawns. Even when they are afraid of the water, even if horses terrify them. They know—yes, everybody knows—that these are the things that mean success.

After Newtown Cunningham, Sam turned the car up a narrow track leading away from the water. As they bumped along over the washboard surface, the round walls of an ancient fort appeared over the brow of the hill. Sam pulled up on the grassy perimeter next to a stone cairn and they got out. As she followed him up the hill she noticed his springy, slightly pigeon-toed walk. The best quarterback in a decade. At the top of the hill Travis stopped and looked back at them. He stretched to his full length, yawned, and then suddenly threw himself end over end in an exuberant cartwheel on the grass.

"Hey, this feels great. I'm glad we came," he said.

Inside the walls, two paths followed the brow of the hill, and galleries opened out from them into the rock. The walls had been rebuilt in places and the new stone seemed harsh and modern next to the mellow, worn, centuries-old surface. It was still a haunted and echoing place. A hawk dipped and floated in the sky.

From the top of the battlements she could see the curving water of Lough Swilly in front of her and the larger inland sea of Lough Foyle on the other side. Green hills with their farmer's patchwork of hay and potatoes sloped softly away from the water and then broke off abruptly in cliffs above the sea. Far away at the end of Lough Foyle, a wooden trawler chugged slowly out to sea.

She looked over at Sam long enough to admire the outline of his hair and features against the soft sky. Below them, Travis tumbled and cartwheeled on the grass. For once he hadn't followed them. She leaned up against Sam and nuzzled his shoulder.

"This is so beautiful," she said. "I'm glad we came." He didn't answer. "Travis seems to be enjoying himself," she went on. As they watched, he did a final somersault and started around the ruin, looking for the stairway.

"We're up here!" Sam called down to him, moving away from her.

"Don't you think it's good for him to be alone sometimes?" she asked. "And for us?" she added in a lower voice.

Sam chose not to hear her. He didn't smile and the muscle in his jaw clenched and unclenched. A vein throbbed slightly under the damp surface of his temple.

"Hey, you guys, let's get going," Travis said, bursting from the walls behind them. "We haven't got all day."

"Okay, let's go," Sam said. He swung around with the resigned determination of a surgeon about to perform a critical operation on a close friend. "I think it will be quicker if we get back on the N–13 and go past Castleford from here."

In the car she tried to relax. As a child she had loved

riding in the car, freed from the responsibilities of homework and chores, swept along the road in the care of her parents. Castleford, Gortlush, Roosky, Bogay. The names had primitive sounds like the cries and grunts of Bronze-Age warriors.

At Killeagh, where they crossed the border, the road was blocked by a police van and three Garda officers in blue uniforms. They were ordered out of the car, and a man examined their passports and papers and the car's registration and rental documents. He scrutinized Hannah's passport and then looked up dispassionately at her face, as if she was an object to be recorded in his memory in case something happened. What could happen? Fear seeped into her mind and the air seemed suddenly heavy and menacing. She remembered now about strip searches and humiliations and innocent travelers being held in foreign jails. It hadn't really occurred to her that they might get hurt. She had the sense of falling through the fragile membrane of security and privilege that had protected her from harm.

So far.

"What is the purpose of your visit?" the man asked.

"We're tourists," Sam said.

The man turned away in disapproving silence. They stood uncomfortably for a minute, their papers clutched in their hands, not knowing what to do next. Finally Sam got back in the car and she and Travis followed him.

About a mile beyond the border they were stopped again.

"I hope it's easier to get out of here than it is to get in," Sam said as he slowed to a halt. She knew it wouldn't be.

Sam rolled down his window and the Garda who had flagged them down ordered them out of the car again. They stood by the side of the road in the raw air as a team of men examined the trunk and the engine. One lay down and shone a beam of light on the undercarriage. Another went through the interior of the car, rooting in the glove compartment and pushing into the leather side pockets on the door. The man-handling of the little car was like a rape.

Another man stood by watching with a German shepherd on a chain leash. "Come on," he ordered them after a while. "This way." He led them about ten yards down the road while the examiners drove the car. These grim, unfriendly men could order them off the road and rip the car apart and ask any questions they wanted. She hoped they were impressed by American passports. Maybe Sam should be trying to bribe them.

They were ordered back into the car this time, and two of the policemen slammed the doors shut on them.

"I hope that's the last one," Sam said.

From the top of the hill after the second checkpoint, they got their first views of Derry. The city was bathed in a soft, pearly light, its great church tower rising above neat rows of brick chimneys. But as they approached, the road was lined with slums and shantytowns. The Bogside. A family of tinkers sat around a fire in an oil barrel in front of a tar-paper lean-to. The girls had brown faces and wore long cotton skirts. Next to them, an emaciated sheep dog with ribs sticking through its matted coat rooted in the dirt. Across the river a squat factory belched smoke out of rusted stacks into the clear air.

At the walls of the city, they passed the first British soldiers, dressed in camouflage gear and flak jackets. A green webbing belt and holster hung from each waist and two of them leaned on shiny black automatic rifles. Their grim faces looked young and smooth. Some still had the traces of adolescent acne or the soft blond down of pubescent beards.

"Holy shit," Travis said. "Some of those guys are younger than I am."

"They're not like you at all, Travis," Sam said. "Don't be silly."

The city was closed to motor vehicles and the soldiers waved them onto a patch of rutted pavement between two Land Rovers. DO NOT GO BEYOND THIS POINT. The great wall of Derry, with its graceful crenelations and pleasant promenade, was a mass of barbed wire. Cinder-block gun emplacements had been built into each indentation of the ramparts.

"I guess my guidebook is a little out of date," Sam said.

"That's for sure," Travis answered. "I wish we'd thought of that sooner."

They walked uphill through the half-deserted streets. Most of the buildings were uninhabited shells; some of their blasted-out windows had been covered with sheets of plywood or cardboard. Did people still live inside, in the darkness? Around the Diamond, where a few shops looked open for business, people hurried along silently, their heads down, their clothes wrapped tightly around them against the wind.

On the other side of the once-graceful central square, a block of buildings had been reduced to rubble: piles of bricks with charred timbers jutting out of them like the arms of drowning men reaching for help that wasn't there. Every unexpected noise—the backfire of a jeep carrying soldiers, Sam kicking a pebble out of the way—went through Hannah like electricity. Her heart pounded.

The brick walls of the ruins beyond the rubble crumbled over and curled like the edge of a piece of paper as it burns. They were covered with white graffiti, some in faded chalk, some in dripping painted letters. *Brits Go Home. Ireland for the Irish. Oh, God, Is There Life Before Death?*

On the way back down the hill they stopped in front of the lighted doorway of a bookshop, one of the few that hadn't been barred up or blasted out. A man leaning on an upended table just inside the entrance eyed them carefully and asked their business. Probably the owner. Too poor to pick up everything and move now, in spite of the troubles. Trying to keep up some semblance of business as usual, and hoping for better times. Trying not to think about what could happen . . . or what had already happened.

Inside the store one small shelf was crowded with conventional books, novels, history, and biography. But most of the space was devoted to racks and racks of books on war. There were serious books on World War I, *Good-Bye to All That* and Sassoon's *Memoirs of an Infantry Officer,* and a lot of books like *The Longest Day* and *Normandy.* In front of these was a big, colorful display of war books for children. Illustrated histories of guns and soldiering, coloring books of war scenes and weapons, reading primers for children whose fathers were in the army. To the side was a rack of war comics; men in flak jackets falling through the air, machine guns blazing their deadly zigzag of red. *Rat-a-tat-tat. Booom, boom, boom.* Screech and thud.

She left Sam pondering over the edition numbers and typefaces of the Graves and Sassoon books, and wandered deeper into the store. A few books of poetry sat on a table at the back. She picked up a paperback volume of *Yeats's* plays and poetry. It was tattered and worn and looked as if it was for borrowing but not for sale. Inside the cover was a torn catalogue card, and someone had turned down a page at the middle of the book. She flipped it open to the dog-eared page, Yeats's epitaph for Jonathan Swift.

Swift has sailed into his rest;
Savage indignation there
Cannot lacerate his breast.
Imitate him if you dare,
World besotted traveller; he
Served human liberty.

Imitate him if you dare. She stared across at the shop wall and the Yeats lines reverberated in her mind. *He served human liberty.*

"Come on, Hannah," Sam said, taking her by the arm from behind. "Let's get out of here." *Imitate him if you dare, world besotted traveller; he. . . .* She put the book back and followed in an obedient daze. *He served human liberty.*

"I hope the car's okay," Sam said.

"That's a funny thing to worry about." Travis's voice was high-pitched and wavery. At each block they passed, a British soldier stood inside a wooden shelter. The road curved around and started back up the hill. They were lost. Sam stopped at one of the shelters and asked the soldier inside how to get back to the bottom of the hill, where the cars were parked. The young man stepped out of his shelter to help—then remembered the rules and stepped back in to get his rifle. Never step into the street unarmed. Do not go beyond this point. *Imitate him if you dare.*

Hannah winced. She had read that the Northern Ireland tour of duty was four months because no one could take it for longer. The soldier looked over at her. He was fair, with a smooth face and bewildered blue eyes. He didn't understand it yet.

"Are you on holiday?" he asked in a dry British accent. I don't know what I'm doing here, his eyes said. I don't know what you're doing here. "Have you had good weather?"

"Yes, yes," she said, "very good weather." She tried to comfort him with her voice, but the look in his eyes was still there when he swiveled away from them and reentered the shelter.

They cut back to the main downhill road through a narrow side street he had pointed out. A row of brick town houses stood empty, their stone stoops covered with debris, plaster, and old boards. More rubble was piled up against the curb. Nobody lived there any more.

The car was all right. Near it, a British soldier in a black beret leaned against his rifle and watched them coldly. But she felt safer inside the car, at least. For a while. They drove out of the city along the river again and crossed a rusting iron bridge over the Foyle. Behind them, the church spire and the tower of the guildhall stood above the old town and the brick houses marched uphill in neat rows again. Ahead, the land was flat and green and the road ran along the curves of the river. But they hadn't left the war. The farmhouses along the A 5 were abandoned and crumbling, and they passed barriers of barbed wire and corrugated sheets of iron along the shoulder. At each crossroads a machine gun poked its sharp, lethal muzzle out of a slit in a sandbag-and-cinder-block shelter. Prehen, Meenaghhill, Bready, and Gortmonly Hill. The sun broke through the low-lying clouds and beat on the cloth roof of the car. It was hot. A bead of sweat stood out on Sam's tanned face below the hairline. His jaw was clenching and unclenching. As she watched him, he slowed down and pulled the car over onto the shoulder.

"What's the matter?"

"I think I'll put the top down, it's turning into a hot day," he said.

"You're kidding!"

"No, I am *not* kidding." There was a scary edge to his voice. "You two wanted to see Northern Ireland, and now you're seeing it. With the top down you can see even more."

He got out and methodically began to unfasten the chrome clips that held the roof of the car to the windshield. She and Travis cowered in their seats. Her own fear had kept her from noticing Sam's anger; now she was terrified by the quiet fury of his actions. Sam was usually so polite that when his temper broke through the surface it seemed unexpected and unfair. She felt like a child being punished. For the first time, she could see how Sam's silent, condescending rage had sent

Travis fleeing across the country and destroyed Nancy's self-esteem.

Sam systematically, determinedly folded back the roof, exposing their reluctant heads to full view.

"I suggest that you try to relax," he said, getting back into the car. "After all, we're tourists on a holiday." Obediently, she tried to relax. She didn't want to argue with a madman. She hunched down in the seat as far as she could without attracting his sarcastic attention. He looked over and gave her a wooden smile.

They drove over to Selma, Alabama, in the big white Buick the group leader had rented in Montgomery. He had planned a day off from canvassing and voter registration to see the sights. A day of tourism. They crossed into town over the bridge where Martin Luther King had joined hands with people from all over the world on his famous march. The back streets of Selma were dirt tracks and stray dogs pawed piles of trash at the curb. The sunken black faces of rural poverty stared out at them from behind rusty screens as they cruised through the outskirts of town. Four fat white people from the North peering out the push-button windows of their fat white air-conditioned car. Sealed in with the outside sealed out. The kid in the front seat tried to get some good rock from the static on the car radio as the leader described the sights.

This is where the troops came in and tear gassed the marchers. This is where Martin Luther King gave his speech. This is the cafe where the Reverend Reeb was clubbed and beaten. The car drew up to the curb. The group leader had arranged for them to have lunch at the cafe. She stared at the dish of eggs and chitlins with grape jelly.

"What's the matter?" the group leader said. "Aren't you hungry?"

The road curved away from the river, and just before they passed through Ballymagorry she heard a strange roaring sound behind them. She was afraid to look around. Sam heard it, too; he slowly pushed his foot down farther on the accelerator. The car sped up, but the noise got louder. Looking over beyond Sam's head, she saw that a black motorcycle was about to pass them on the narrow roadway. The driver was dressed in black with a black helmet, his eyes hidden behind heavy goggles. He drew abreast of them, staring right into the car from above as his machine raced down the center of the asphalt. For a moment he just watched as they looked helplessly back up at his masked face. Then his thick lips twisted up in an obscene smirk and he sped ahead, vanishing around a curve in the road.

The route bent back across the fields toward the river as they approached Strabane. In town, all traffic was permanently detoured around the main square. The village green was a patch of torn-up mud, and the great oaks which once shaded it had been sawed off at the ground, their amputated stumps covered with black tar. A square cement bunker commanded the road and a brown armored tank was backed up next to it, its machine gun moving back and forth in a slow, searching arc. Across the street there were faded signs where the butcher and the baker had once had their shops at the edge of a pleasant, tree-shaded Irish village green. A weathered plaque with a pitcher of beer painted on it hung from one hinge in front of the abandoned pub.

On the other side of town, where the road crossed the river, she could see the border. At last. A wall of gates and plywood planking was topped with swirls of barbed wire. Traffic backed up toward town from the exit checkpoint, where soldiers were stopping and searching each car. Just a few more minutes. There were five cars in the line already, so they would be the sixth. It couldn't take too long. But instead of heading for their place in the line, Sam turned the car left down a road that ran south along the river.

"What are you doing?" The river was an opaque brown

band running slowly between flat muddy banks. Snags and tangles of brush interrupted the surface of the water. Sam didn't answer.

"Hey, how come we aren't getting in line?" She tried to keep her voice calm.

He turned to her with an expression of absolute unconcern. "Don't you remember?" he said evenly. "We planned to have lunch down here. There's a place on the river Frederick told me about. I know I mentioned it to you."

"Couldn't we skip it?"

"No, we could not skip it," Sam said. The border receded behind them. "This is the plan we all agreed on, and we're going to follow it."

Sam and his plans. When Sam was afraid, he didn't know what to do but stick faithfully to his plans. He held his careful arrangements in front of him like a shield. It was as if he thought that adhering to something he had controlled —the plans—would enable him to extend that control to real circumstances. And when Sam was angry, he used his plans against other people. He couldn't take their feelings into account because, after all, there were the plans to be considered. If they ruined his plans, as Travis had done, they failed him.

They drove in silence along the edge of the river until they came to a line of ramshackle houses tilted against the bank.

"This is it," Sam said. A torn and faded awning jutted from one of the facades. Pat's Cafe, the awning said, except that the P, the t and the C were missing. Below it, the peeling front of yellow stucco was weathered to a dingy gray. Two doors indicated it had been built as a double house, but it looked as if many more than two families had lived there at one time or another. The foundation was cracked, and the whole building sagged dangerously in the direction of the river.

"It looks a little shabby, but Frederick said it would be fine," Sam said. Anyway, she thought angrily, it's in the plan. There could be a cordon of armed men around the place and we'd still have to stop for lunch. The plan proposes and the plan disposes.

Sam knocked at the left-hand door. Nothing happened. Standing there, she felt certain they were being examined by eyes from behind the torn curtains on the second floor. Sam knocked again. The flimsy wooden door was opened from inside, shrieking on a rusty hinge. The shadow of a woman appeared through the screen. She was wearing a faded cotton housedress and her gray hair was pulled back in a ragged bun. She shook her head at them to send them away.

"There's no one here," she said in a rasping brogue. "What would you be wanting?" She gave the impression that she was about to slam the door.

Sam smiled politely. "But my friend Frederick Culloden said I could get a bite to eat here," he said in a smooth, flattering voice. "He said you serve the best lamb stew in all of Ireland."

The woman opened the screen a crack and her face seemed less harsh. There probably wasn't a female in the world who wouldn't be thawed out by Sam's good looks and his attentive manner.

"Oh, it's Culloden that sent you. Well, I guess you had better come in." With a trace of friendliness she pushed the door all the way, another shriek, and ushered them into a dank parlor. Huge faded cabbage roses on the wallpaper bubbled off the wall from the dampness. A sofa with a pattern of cigarette burns across the grimy flowered fabric was pushed up against a closed door, and on the table next to the lamp a dozen old butts rotted in the dregs of a Pepsi bottle.

"We'll see what we can do for you," the woman said. "It's late." They followed her across the room. The back of her housedress had been patched with different fabrics, her stockings were rolled to just above her ankles, and her slippers flapped around yellowed heels. She opened another door and led them onto a porch above the river that had not been visible from the road. The boards creaked and the posts of the building bowed out, but the porch jutted out over the river where it curved away from Strabane. For a moment it seemed as if they were far away. Sheep grazed in a meadow on the other side. There were three tables on the slanting floor, set with green glasses and heavy linen napkins soft from hundreds of washings. At one table near the other end, two burly men were spooning thick stew onto crusty slices of bread.

"This looks fine," Sam said, settling down in a chair with his back to the door. She sat down. Travis sat down.

"I'll bring you some stew," the woman said. "That's all there is."

"Thank you very much," Sam said.

They waited in tense silence. After a short, mumbled conversation, the other two diners got up and left the porch by the door at the other end. Their half-eaten plates of stew were still hot, wisps of steam from the fragrant brown lumps of lamb curled up and vanished into the raw river air.

When their bowls of stew came, the woman plunked them down without ceremony, serving Sam first. The meat was warm and well seasoned, but after one bite the smells of the river overwhelmed its taste. Damp mud and sour earth. Rats probably lived in those reeds along the water. Across the porch the abandoned bowls of stew were beginning to congeal and glaze around the edges. A forkful of meat went down Hannah's throat and settled like a rock in her stomach. Her appetite was gone. Next to her, Travis listlessly pushed his meat around the bowl with his fork.

"What's the matter?" Sam asked. "Aren't you hungry?"

182

Finally it was over. Sam paid with a roll of Irish pounds, peeling the green notes off the thick wad, and they walked back out to the car. As they got in, she felt eyes from the second floor scrutinizing every move. With the top of the car down, the interior was entirely exposed—gleaming leather seats and soft black carpeting and the whorls in the grain on the wooden gearshift knob. They still had to cross the border. The piece of meat she had eaten lay undissolved in her gut. Cold wind whipped at them as Sam turned the car around in a U-turn on the empty road and headed back up the river.

This time only two cars were ahead of them in the line, a gray van and a dilapidated Morris Mini. They waited with the engine idling as the soldiers checked every inch of the van. Behind them a man drew up in a blue pickup truck. It looked like a commandeered farm vehicle and its driver stared at them with open fascination, his black eyes taking in every aspect of their appearance. The girl, the elegant man, the young man, and the obscenely fancy little convertible. His gaze from behind made her squirm. When Sam finally drove into the checkpoint, she pulled down the handle to get out.

"Wait a second," he said, and grabbed her arm roughly.

"Passports," the officer demanded. Sam showed their trio of royal-blue U.S. passports and the grim soldier waved them past impatiently. More damn-fool sightseers. None of them talked on the way back to Ballymarr.

Hannah slept for the rest of the afternoon, a hot, depressed, dreamless sleep between sweaty sheets. Relief overwhelmed her. A great, irresistible tiredness replaced her tension. The naked lives and the ruined countryside faded in her memory. Sam dozed for a while next to her, but when she woke up he was gone. She flopped over onto his side of the bed in a stretch and went back to sleep.

"Come on, Hannah," he was saying as he stood over her the next time she woke up. "It's time for dinner."

Even at dinner she was exhausted. It felt as if her body had plugged into the need for all the sleep she had missed in the past ten days. She couldn't wait to get back to bed. If it weren't for the trouble it would cause, she would have rested her head on the table and dozed off. Or plopped her forehead into the soup the way she heard F. Scott Fitzgerald did at the Murphys' in Antibes one night. The snippy polite conversation bounced off her mind like high-velocity cotton balls.

"Could you pass the bread?"

"Would you like some more vegetables?"

"Wine?"

"Butter, please, Travis."

"Coffee, Hannah? Hannah, would you like some coffee?"

Yes, yes, yes, and yes. Sam was clearly willing to pretend that the day hadn't happened. There had been no fear, no disasters, no quiet hatred between them. He and Travis seemed to be getting along well enough that way. For the moment, though, everything was too much for her. She didn't understand. She just wanted to go to sleep.

Chapter

22

She rolled over, eye-level with the sheets. Sam's place next to her in the bed was empty, a pattern of dents in the linen like the rumples a wave leaves at the tide line on soft sand. The sounds of forks clinking against plates, and the smells of coffee and toast drifted up to her from the dining room below. He was letting her sleep.

She pushed her back into the mattress and stretched her arms up above her head, letting her muscles tighten and relax up and down the length of her body. It felt good. Yesterday was over. The trip into Northern Ireland was already fading in her memory. It would be an interesting story, back in New York. For now, she was happy to be alone for a few minutes, outside the daily schedule of the castle and the inexorable pressure of Sam's plans.

Her mind drifted back to New York. After her divorce, she had been so afraid of being alone. When Joe had left, a great void yawned terrifyingly at the center of her life. How would she ever fill up that time? Daily rounds, appointments, routines had saved her. Nights and weekends were the hardest. But as she had gotten further away from the divorce, slowly the time had begun to vanish and soon she was as busy and frantic without Joe as she had been with him. Still, underneath it, she sometimes remembered that panicky feeling of a life without structure.

Maybe that was the way Sam felt all the time. Maybe he was a study in controlled panic. What control. Maybe he was afraid that if he broke down or even relaxed, the whole facade of his life would just collapse around him. Brick and plaster crumbling against the internal walls like a building in an earthquake.

When she pushed against Sam's limits, though, or when circumstances did, he just got angry. Like yesterday. Instead of admitting that he was afraid, too, he had turned on them. Was that because he was so much older? After all, when she counted up, she was closer to Travis's age than she was to Sam's. She was still looking forward to everything. Sam was old and locked in a lifetime of patterns.

Now, lying alone, she dreaded returning to the predictability of her life in New York. She was sick of being on time, on schedule, on *it*. "I'm on it," they would say at the office, or "get on it." Now she felt like getting off it. She was young, she was single, she was healthy, she could do anything or go anywhere. She could marry a gillie and raise his children and become a Catholic wife. She could quit Barter Books and arranging promotion for ungrateful authors and writing press releases, and go off and be a waitress in Aspen and ski every day if she wanted to. Nothing was holding her back. She could go west as Travis had. Or she could go back across the border and join the fight for Irish independence. She could serve human liberty. If she dared.

"When are you going to settle down?" the psychiatrist said. "You're so bright, but you haven't learned to take your own life seriously."

"That's why I'm here." This was always a good answer.

186

She swung her legs down over the side of the bed and sat up. Enough of that. She dressed and went down to the dining room, concentrating on acting sober-sided and grown-up. But the wildness in her heart persisted. Sam looked as glamorous as ever, sipping his coffee and reading the *Irish Times* that the hotel delivered especially for him. He looked up at her with a smile, willing to forget yesterday. No I-told-you-so's. But he was old. There were wrinkles on his neck and the skin was papery and crinkled along the underside of his arms. His hair was speckled with gray and his fingernails had started to split when he forgot to put lotion on them. Hemorrhoids and a touch of arthritis, ear wax and incipient gum disease. A man in his fifties was no bargain.

She sat down and ordered her breakfast.

"What's up for today, gang?" Travis burst into the room like a blast of summer wind. His shirt was half-buttoned and his hair still tousled from sleep. "Great! I was afraid I might have missed breakfast."

"Well, we're up, and quite a bit earlier than you, I might add," Sam said. Travis sprawled in his chair and reached for the silver toast rack.

"Pass the butter please, Dad. It looks like a terrific day." He was mumbling now, because his mouth was full of toast.

"Better than yesterday," she said.

"You can say that again."

"I thought maybe we'd just rest up today," Sam said. He actually sounded apologetic about not having planned a trip. "I have a lot of reading and letter-writing to catch up on, anyway. I've got to drive into town this morning and get the London papers and do some errands. Want to come?" He looked over at her as he stood up. His breakfast was finished and he was ready to go. She was still eating her eggs and bacon.

"Would you mind if I didn't, Sam? I'm still eating." Sam

wanted her company, but she didn't feel like getting back in the car with him. Not quite yet.

"Okay, see you later."

With Sam gone, she relaxed and helped herself to another big piece of toast. Travis was just digging into the double order of eggs and sausages and broiled tomatoes which had come out of the kitchen.

"I see you've gotten over your temporary loss of appetite," she said.

"Mmmm, I didn't like that at all."

"It was awful," she agreed. "Jam, please."

Sam appeared in the doorway with his sweater looped over his shoulders and waved goodbye. She had finished eating as much as she should have, but she didn't get up to go with him. Enjoying every moment, she spread homemade strawberry jam from a little white dish onto the extra piece of toast.

"How did you get mixed up with Dad?" Travis asked.

The question caught her with her mouth full. "I met him at a party in New York," she said finally.

"Some hotsy-totsy publishing party, I bet."

"Not really, just a cocktail thing for an author in one of those rooms at the St. Regis."

"Unh-huh."

"Okay, I guess in New York we take a lot of things for granted."

"So, did he sweep you off your feet right there at the party? Or did he use his slow, hypnotic method?"

She laughed. "The slow one, I guess. How come?"

"Oh, nothing really. It's just that you're not like his other girls at all." Travis had finished his eggs and he mopped up the residue of yolk and butter with a piece of bread.

"You mean not so chic, don't you?"

Now Travis laughed. "Well, he does seem to go for

188

models, but it's a whole lot more than that. It just doesn't seem as if he's your type exactly."

"Thanks."

"It's a compliment."

They got up from the table and walked out through the french doors to the terrace. The sun felt hot through her clothes. Travis had a lot of nerve, asking her these questions that were basically none of his business. She probably shouldn't be talking to him about Sam at all. Anything she said might be used against her if things got tense again. They sat down together on the flagstones, leaning up against the stone bench.

"Well, what do you think *is* my type?" she asked. Her voice sounded slightly reproving.

"Don't be sore," he said. "It's just that I could see you with someone sort of younger, more adventurous maybe."

"No, I'm really not angry. It's interesting to know what impression you give to other people. But more adventurous? Like an explorer or a stunt man?"

"Not like *that*. It's just, well, maybe he seems sort of older and authoritarian to me because he's my father."

"Maybe you're jealous."

"I *have* hurt your feelings—I'm sorry." It sounded as if he really was sorry, not just apologizing to make things run smoothly the way his father did.

"No, that's okay." She looked out at the river. Travis was probably right anyway, even though it made her uncomfortable to talk about it with him. In New York Sam's age had seemed irrelevant. A lot of girls she knew had married much older men and no one mentioned it—especially if the man was as rich and as attractive as Sam. But here everything seemed different. Her perception started to shift. Sam's age, after all, was a fact. For now it was all right. But when she was Sam's age, still full of life and energy, he would be seventy-plus. Probably a pretty querulous seventy, too. Sam was one of those men who would never be able to understand why old age had to happen to *him*. And old age was a shipwreck.

With an older man, a man like Sam, she would have to fit into his life, accept his upsetting past, go where he went, and get along with his friends. He was too old to change. Sam had had his child, he was set in his ways and didn't have the energy to start that all over again. With a younger man there would be shared adventures, shared decisions. They could do whatever they liked. There would be no stifling ties to families and no obligations of a successful career. They could have children of their own.

She took the pack of cigarettes out of her pocket and lit one for herself. A long inhale. Smoking brought her back to earth, scorching her throat and blunting her fantasies. She held the harsh smoke in her lungs for a moment and then breathed out, relaxing in the sun.

"I wish you wouldn't smoke," Travis said.

"Talk about authoritarian!"

"It's okay to be authoritarian when you're right."

They sat in uncomfortable silence now. She kept on smoking. Currents of doubt and anger revived and echoed between them. She was relieved to hear Sam's car come up the drive, and she got up and walked around the terrace to meet him with a kiss.

Chapter

23

At lunch the doors were open onto the terrace and sweet warm air blew through the dining room. The heavy scent of roses and heather was intoxicating, and Hannah felt light-headed and happy. Spring fever weather. Sam had ordered a bottle of Pouilly-Fumé and the pale-yellow liquid buzzed in her veins.

"Why don't we take a nap after lunch?" she said, smiling at him as suggestively as she dared while Travis's attention was distracted. She slipped off her sandal under the table and pressed the inside of Sam's calf with her foot.

"I'm kind of sleepy, as a matter of fact," Sam said. "I had some trouble sleeping last night." That wasn't what she meant, but it was good enough. Once she got him to the bedroom alone, she would turn his mind on to sexual things. Visions of a delirious summer afternoon between the sheets danced in her head as she followed him upstairs. She opened the bedroom windows to let in the honeyed summer smells and quickly took off her clothes, arranging her nude body under the sheets in a disheveled, irresistible pose. A soft breeze blew across the bed, caressing her skin as she lay there waiting. Sam stripped down to his boxer shorts and lay down next to her. She nuzzled his neck and chest and stroked his stomach.

"Sweet Hannah," he crooned, "let's not be angry with each other." He rolled toward her and took her in his arms, kissing her gently on the forehead and adjusting his body so that it fitted comfortably against her.

"You're wonderful, Sam," she said, blowing gently into his warm ear and arching her back toward him. She waited, her excitement beginning to rise, murmuring to him, for his response. She waited for his hand to slip down her lower back and caress her there. Or for him to push his hips forward against her to let her feel his erection. But as she held him, his soft breathing changed subtly, and in a moment she heard him sighing the deep breaths of sleep. Naptime. Sweet old Sam. She cradled his body in her arms.

She tried to sleep. But the seductive afternoon air eddying around her body made her restless. Her mind raced. She wanted to be outdoors, playing and walking and enjoying the day. There weren't many days like this. Quietly she untangled herself from the sheets and got up. She put on her jeans and a shirt and sandals and softly closed the bedroom door on slumbering Sam. Downstairs she slipped her copy of *Tess* out of the bookshelves and walked out through the doors to the terrace.

Travis was already there. He looked up.

"Oh, good! I was afraid you were out of commission for the afternoon. What happened to Dad?"

"He's asleep." She tried not to sound chagrined.

"But it's too nice a day to sleep—it's so wonderful out here. Conor says this weather is very rare."

"I know, the air is fantastic."

"Want to take a walk? When I was talking to him before,

Conor told me there's a ruined castle on this property, on the other side of the woods. We could go and have a look."

"Deal," she said.

They crunched across the gravel and down through the archway that led to the fishing water. At first they walked in Indian file along the river. Trout leapt from the glassy surface in blue and silver arcs. The air was like a warm compress on her forehead.

"He told me how to get there," Travis said. "There should be a bridge along here somewhere."

They crossed the footbridge, a rustic wooden construction of unplaned planks with log railings, and took a path toward the lough, walking on a carpet of coppery pine needles. The path branched to the left and Travis paused for a moment, then took the right fork.

"There are a lot of paths back here," he said.

"Have you walked back here before?"

"Just that time I came back from the beach," he said. "Otherwise I wouldn't go off the path. I have a lousy sense of direction. I mean really lousy."

"I hope you aren't getting us lost."

"No, I think this is right."

The path widened as it penetrated a grove of beeches. The sun coming through their pale-green leaves made a moving pattern on the ground, and the fragrance of the pines around them filled the air. Underneath that she could smell the salty, earthy smell that means the nearness of the sea. The pinewoods on Cape Cod. You cross the Bourne Bridge and you're there. There in the middle of summer days and long picnics and lying on the beach feeling sleepy and sunburned. American summer days with their bright mornings and peach-pie sunsets and quick, friendly love affairs.

Now the path turned into an abandoned road through the woods and they walked along together. Travis easily adjusted his long stride to hers. They didn't talk. A meadow appeared through the screen of the last trees along the road, and she saw the old castle ahead of them, a stone circle sitting on top of the knoll like a gray crown.

"Hey, there it is!" she said.

They clambered up the grassy rise and found themselves standing on a narrow ledge at the bottom of the ruin. Its wall, a gridwork of huge gray stones, was smooth and high, and its worn surface offered no apparent footholds.

"Doesn't look good," she said.

"There must be a way in." Travis began stepping his way around the wall to the right and she followed him. It was hard to keep from falling off the ledge back onto the hill as they moved. One step forward. Cling to the wall and bring the other foot even. The stones felt pleasantly cool against her face and hands as they inched their way along. The sun warmed her back.

About halfway around the enclosure, just as she had started to think that perhaps there was no way in, the flat stones gave way to a high arch with a carved shield set at its peak, and they walked through to the inside. The floor was a level grassy meadow, finer and softer than the grass on the knoll. The crumbling walls of an old foundation pushed out of the grass in one corner. All around them the gray walls rose straight up from the ground, as hermetic now that they were inside as they had been unyielding when they were outside. They blocked out the view of the surrounding landscape and created an absolute stillness. Silence echoed off them. It was a magic enclosure, a faraway place, faraway even from the rest of Ireland. They sat down on the grass to the left of the archway.

"It's like a secret garden," she said.

"Maybe. It's kind of spooky in here, though."

"But it's so beautiful, like being inside one of those candy Easter eggs, frozen in time and space."

194

"Conor says it's haunted."

"Come on."

"No, really, he says there's a story about it, about the wife of the man who built Ballymarr leaving him and moving over here with another man or something."

"Does he think that's enough to make it haunted?" Hannah laughed. "In that case, an awful lot of places are haunted."

"No, no." Travis laughed, too. "The way he told it, something terrible happened . . . I mean more terrible than that. Let's see, it was something like that the man who built Ballymarr ordered them to leave here. I mean her and the other man. And they were going to, and then there was a big fire and the place burned down and they disappeared."

"Does anyone know where they went? They probably lived happily ever after somewhere else."

"No, that's the spooky part. The bodies were never found and no one saw them leave either. Conor says there are a lot of stories about them but that people around here believe that they died in the fire and still come back as ghosts. He says there are some people who have claimed to see her, walking in these woods or on the local roads. She'll appear by the side of the road, and if a car stops for her, she's suddenly not there."

It was spooky. These woods. A slow tingle raised the roots of her hair and a delicious shiver prickled her back and arms.

"See, it even gives you gooseflesh," he said, pointing to the tiny bumps that appeared on her forearm.

"Do you believe in ghosts?" she asked.

"When I want to," he said. "Sure."

The sun was still warm and the thrill of fear faded as she stretched out in it, savoring the texture of the grass and the springy ground.

Travis sprawled out next to her, leaning on his elbow. She

noticed the watch on his wrist and she felt an unpleasant chill of anger and resentment.

"It's funny," he was saying, "this place reminds me of a rock formation in Utah near Canyonlands where we used to camp sometimes when I was out there. The cowboys used it as a corral because there was only one opening in the rock circle, sort of a natural version of this."

"You must have seen a lot," she said. "I've never even been out west."

"Oh, well." He shrugged it off but he sounded pleased. "I guess so."

"Life out there must have been pretty interesting."

He smiled, acknowledging the flattery in her questions. "Yeah. The West is really different. Sometimes the East seems like a silly kind of place after the experience I had out there." He was boasting.

"I bet you left a trail of broken hearts across Colorado and Utah," she said.

"Oh, it's not really like that," he said. "It really isn't. That's what I mean about the difference. I was moving around so much that I didn't have time for real girl friends." He looked self-consciously sad. "I've had a lot of women, I guess you could say, but not too many girl friends."

"Only about fifty?" she teased. "Only about a hundred?"

He laughed. "Not exactly." He rolled over on his stomach and rested his head against his arms. The smooth bones of his wrist came to rest in the grass just in front of her. Sun winked off the gold beveling of the watch.

"Well, it had to be a girl friend who gave you that cute stuffed monkey that was riding in your pack when you arrived," she said.

He looked across and up at her. "You notice everything, don't you? That was Callie. She was a girl at the ranch where I worked."

196

"And?"

"Well, she was the daughter of the owner, and I guess they both sort of thought I would stay on." He rolled back up on his elbow and looked at the castle wall. The watch glistened a few inches away from her own hand resting on the ground.

"That's such a beautiful watch," she said.

"Yeah, isn't it nice? It's Dad's, though, I have to remember to give it back to him. Maybe if I play it right he'll buy me another one."

"Let's see." She reached over and turned Travis's wrist to expose the buckle. Using both hands, she bent over him to undo it and slip it out toward her. He was watching.

"Can I help?" he said. Gently he buckled the watch onto her smaller wrist. She spread her hands out on the grass, kneeling back to see how it looked. Beneath them she could almost feel the deep rhythms of the earth throbbing just below the surface. The heartbeat of the world. Maybe she and Travis would end up being friends after all. Sam was too cold to deal with him. She had been warm and receptive enough to break through his protective shell.

Now he reached out and touched her shoulder, and his hand sent tingling little electric shocks across her chest and down her legs. Her body felt weak and she sank lower on her knees. Travis looked right into her eyes.

"I want you," he said. His voice was much lower. "I want you badly." He leaned toward her, forcing her over onto her side on the grass.

"Travis!" Her voice sounded as surprised as she felt. He was looming over her now, cradling her head in his hands and looking down at her with love and intensity. "Come on, don't do that!" She tried to pull away from him, but her resistance thawed in the hot force of his desire. She could see his erection pushing out against the fabric of his jeans, and feel the weight of his body on top of her. His lust excited her, his panting loosened her thighs. There was no ambivalence or doubt in Travis. He wanted her. He wanted to fuck her and ravish her and have her right now on the grass. She tried to push at him again, but he held her more tightly, pressing one of his legs between her knees to open her up to him.

"You want it, too," he said. "You want it, too." His face was smooth and flushed and he smelled of the sweet grass. He kissed her neck, and the roots of her hair tingled. He was right. She wanted it, too, now. So much.

"Listen, Trav," she said, trying to control the hot breath which blurred her voice, "you know this isn't a good idea."

"What do I care about ideas?" He was unbuttoning the top of her shirt now. "I want you and you want me. Come on, come on," he moaned. How could she say no to him now? He knelt above her with his knees between her legs, stroking the tops of her breasts. He wanted her so much. Then her shirt was off and he was pushing at her hard nipples with his hands and smiling down at her.

"You want it, too." She didn't protest any more. He undid the snap and zipper of her pants and pulled them down around her hips and she felt the ground cool against her naked skin. He knew just what to do. He spread her legs open and felt inside her to where she was damp and warm and ready for him and then he pulled off his own pants and his cock was big and stiff and sure as he leaned over her and slid it in, moving up and down.

"I want you to come, I want you to come," he was saying, and then she was. Up and over and colors dancing under her closed eyelids and flooded with that inner light. And then he came, too, with a long soft groan. Oh, yes, he said, oh yes, oh yes. And then they were lying there together, two half-naked people on the grass with the late-afternoon shadows gathering around them.

He kissed her cheek and pulled up her pants and buttoned her shirt as if she were a child.

"I don't want you to get chilled," he said.

She gazed glassy-eyed up at the sky, her body still warm with satisfaction, her mind a hazy blank. Slowly the full feeling of sex ebbed away from her and her mind began to clear. She felt cold and exposed. Remorse and chagrin began their icy work.

Travis was sprawled on the grass again in an attitude of total relaxed satisfaction. His eyes were closed, but he was smiling, as if he expected her to leap on him at any moment and want it all over again. No second thoughts for him. He did what he wanted to do. No confusion, no complexity, no post-coital sadness.

She turned toward him and sat up. "Well, what now?" she said, more to herself than to him. Her voice sounded anxious and prudish. Travis opened his eyes and smiled at her, reaching his arms above his head for a stretch.

"Hunh?" he said.

"You know, what do we do now?" she insisted.

"Heavy." He threw his voice into the second syllable, drawing it out like a groan. "I don't know, whatever you want, I guess."

There was a vast space between them. She was talking about moral standards and the salvation of her soul and the rest of her life. He was wondering whether they should do it again right now, or go back to the hotel and have dinner and then do it again.

"I guess at the moment we had better go back to the hotel," she said.

"Are you angry with me or something?" A shadow flickered in his eyes.

"No, it's not you. I'll be okay, Trav. Come on."

He got up and brushed the grass off his clothes. The sun had set behind the top of the wall now, and the warm afternoon had turned cold. She shivered in the thin shirt.

"Here, wear my sweater," he said. "Don't get cold."

Obediently, she pulled the soft blue shetland on over her shirt. It was warm and smelled of Travis and the grass and summer afternoons. If only she could enjoy it. But regret and guilt flowered in her heart. *Agenbite of inwit;* agenbite, you nitwit. How could she have been so stupid? Sam had brought her here, she was Sam's girl, and she was with Sam. "Doesn't he know that you're here with me?" he had asked when Jake wanted to take her back to Paris.

Of course, she had never promised Sam anything, and he had never asked—nor volunteered any promises of his own. Still, she had broken a promise anyway. If Sam knew what had happened, he would mind. Mind? He would be hurt and furious and turned off. And he would be right.

"It's time you learned to take responsibility for your actions," the doctor said. "These things have consequences even if you pretend to ignore them."

The doctor was right, too. What had happened with Travis was the consequence of her fantasies and restlessness this morning and her frustration with Sam after lunch. She hadn't had the courage to tell Sam how she was feeling, so she punished him in secret. Now her dreams seemed childish and stupid. She didn't want to run off with a gillie or be a cocktail waitress. She was doing what she wanted in New York. Maybe she could have a better job, but she was happy in the community of writers and editors and people who cared about books. And the men she liked were part of this community: Joe and David and Sam. They were men she could talk to. Men who shared her own ideas and concerns, men who had been seasoned by knowledge and experience.

And Sam was an aristocrat in this world. He had read more and seen more than the rest of them. He was what she wanted, the top of the line, best of breed, the prize. If she had wanted to fuck around with a boy or be a cocktail waitress or a gillie's wife, she would have. Nothing was stopping her.

Walking beside her with his arm looped over her shoulders, Travis made her feel old. His shirt was folded back on his forearm, exposing a faint stripe of white where the watch had been. He leaned down and picked a pinecone off the forest floor and threw it up in the air, running forward and underneath to catch it behind his back. Showing off. Animal energy, high spirits. Her spirits sank as they walked up the driveway. Her throat felt dry.

"Let's not say anything about this," she said. "Let's keep it a secret." She forced herself to give his arm a conspiratorial squeeze although it was hard for her even to touch him without feeling revulsion for what they had done.

"Okay, whatever you want is okay with me," he said. His obliviousness was unruffled. Claustrophobia descended on her like a choking cloud. Why was he so willing? Didn't he ever question anything? She walked faster so that she would be ahead of him as they crossed the driveway. In case Sam was watching. She wanted it to look as if they weren't really together, but he followed her through the doors.

The gloom in the hallway seemed darker. At one end of it the flickering glow of firelight outlined the door to the library. She approached quickly in the halfhearted hope that Travis would decide to go upstairs, or to the bar, or anywhere else but after her. Through the doorway she saw that Sam was writing letters. The evening had turned cool and Sam looked just right, working in front of an early fire, in his tweed jacket. His wavy head was bent over the leather surface of the desk, and his jacket fell through the arms of the Chippendale side chair. He was at home, to the manor and the manner born. But when he looked up and saw them standing in the doorway his face seemed to freeze.

"Oh, there you are," he said. His voice caught in his throat for a split second. "Conor was looking for you, Travis. Where have you two been?"

A deep blush betrayed her; maybe he wouldn't notice in this light. "Oh, we just went for a walk," she said. "We went down to a ruined castle that Conor told Travis about. It was fantastic. I wish you had come."

She moved sideways to disassociate herself from Travis. Automatically, he ambled over and stood beside her. She flashed on their image, the scene could have been Travis asking Sam for her hand in marriage. What a farce! Now she was talking too much, too fast. Did Sam notice that she was wearing the blue sweater? What would he think when he saw that she had the watch back? She would have to work out a story about how she had told Travis how much it meant to her because of Sam. And how, when he understood, he had given it back.

For the moment, the thing was to get away from Travis so they didn't look so much like a couple. She didn't even trust him not to put a proprietary paw on her shoulder. She smiled at Sam and crossed the room toward his chair. He stood up quickly as she approached, knocking his pen off the desk. He stepped away from her to retrieve it, keeping the chair safely between them.

"I'm going upstairs to change for dinner," he said, gathering up his letters and heading for the door.

"Wait, Sam, I'm coming, too." At the door she stopped and turned back toward Travis. She frowned and put a finger to her lips. He blew her a kiss.

24

Sam moved around the bedroom getting ready for dinner. From the bureau to the bed, from the bed to the bureau. As she stripped off her shirt and pants to take a bath, she wondered how he could avoid noticing the rich, salty smell of sex on her skin. The room reeked of her transgression. Even with the window open, the night smells were no match for the heavy perfume of sweat and semen that billowed from her pores. She waited until Sam seemed preoccupied with the laces of his shoes, then she quickly stuffed Travis's blue sweater into a bottom drawer behind some old shirts that she hadn't worn.

"I'm going to take a bath before dinner," she said.

"Fine." His voice was cool and even. "I'll meet you down there."

She crossed the hall to the bathroom and shut the door behind her, pushing the bolt across it to lock herself in. She looked in the mirror. Same old face. In the bathtub she would wash the whole afternoon away. The smells of sex, the excitement of a new man, the hurt to Sam. Out damn Travis.

All the perfumes of Arabia; she wished she could pour them into the bubbling water coming from the faucet. She would forget what had happened and maybe Sam would forget, too. His methodical silence was worse than a direct accusation. When she got back across the hall, the bedroom was empty. She put on her gray skirt and a somber black sweater and walked downstairs. She would match Sam's dignity. They would be the grown-ups, and Travis would be the child.

As she took her place, she noticed that two new guests had been seated at the table behind her chair. They were both dark-haired men with broad working-class faces, and they dug into their food with unmannerly gusto. They looked a little like the two men she and Sam and Travis had seen on the porch at Pat's Cafe, that horrible place in Strabane. One wore a shiny black gabardine suit and the other one had on a badly fitting tweed jacket that drooped off his shoulders. They looked up at her with open curiosity as she tucked her skirt under herself and sat down. A little rude. What were two men like that doing at a place like Ballymarr, anyway?

Sam was drinking a martini and Travis had a beer. When the waitress came, she ordered iced tea—no need to have her tongue loosened any more than it already was. Travis was sitting next to her, and as he reached in front of her place for the bread, she prayed that Sam wouldn't notice the casual way he brushed against her shoulder.

"I understand some men went out today and got a couple of salmon," Sam said.

"Really."

"I didn't know you could catch salmon in this river," Travis said, turning toward his father. They had finished the soup and were waiting for the lamb chops. She felt Travis's free right hand slipping under the edge of her skirt and onto her knee beneath the level of the table. She tried to move her leg, but the table leg was in the way. His hand inched up her thigh.

"Had you thought about fishing for salmon, Dad?" He began to manipulate his fingers around the edge of her underpants. She was terrified. Trapped like an animal caught in the headlights of an oncoming car. The next course was put in front of them and Travis brought his hand back up to the table to eat.

"I thought about it, but you need a different kind of equipment," Sam said.

"Wouldn't it be worth it?" There were two lamb chops on each plate. Travis had barely finished one of his when she felt his hand lifting her skirt again.

"I don't know about more equipment at this point," Sam was saying. "I don't think we'll be staying here much longer. Have you thought about doing some more traveling before you head for home?" Slowly, inexorably, Travis's hand slid up her thigh. There was nothing she could do about it.

"Not really. What are your plans?" Travis asked.

"We'll probably go south, but maybe you should see more of France or even Italy while you're over here. Could we have another bottle of white wine, please?" Sam had polished off two martinis and this was the second bottle of wine. The liquor was beginning to slow down his voice, and she noticed the slight misalignment of his eyes that happened when he was tired or a little drunk. Good.

"I wish I knew as much about wine as you did, Dad," Travis said, kneading her flesh between his fingers. He obviously liked feeling her up under the table while he talked to Sam. Maybe the whole thing had to do with Sam. She was just an adjunct to their passionate and complex love-hate knots. He wasn't fucking *her* this afternoon, he was fucking *Sam*.

"It's a shame for you to spend all this time in Europe and

only see a small part of Ireland," Sam said. "What's happened to your appetite, Travis? I thought the lamb chops were pretty good." Travis brought his hand back up above the table and started on his second chop.

"I'm trying not to eat so fast," he explained glibly. "I heard somewhere it's better for you." But as the plates were cleared away she felt his hand again, this time on the outside of her thigh, slipping relentlessly toward its goal. She looked nervously around for the waitress, hoping that dessert would come quickly and distract Travis once again. Maybe she could excuse herself soon, pleading a headache. Behind their chairs her gaze was caught by one of the men at the next table. They had apparently finished, and they were both leaning back and leering at her.

As she looked, one of them puckered up his lips in an obscene sucking pantomime and the other one laughed grossly. Suddenly she realized that from their vantage point they could watch what was happening under her table. Travis's hand was hidden from Sam, but these two men had seen what was happening. Now they slobbered and slurped in disgusting amusement, as if they were thinking about what they would do to her if she was with them. She felt a flash of heat and nausea and she stood up, knocking her chair back onto the floor.

"I think I'll take a walk, I don't feel well," she said. Flaming with embarrassment and shame, she hurried out of the dining room, leaving the waitress to pick up her chair. The lecherous guffaws of the two men echoed in her head as she walked down the hall and out onto the gravel.

Walking cooled her off. They would leave now. The fairy-tale dream of Ballymarr had been shattered. The place had seemed so pure, so remote from grubbiness and malice, but she had brought the shadows of violence and sex down upon them. The green-eyed monster jealousy, the demanding serpent of sex. It was like the men coming to the island in the boat in *Victory*. Axel Heyst had gone there with the girl and everything was fine until the men in the boat had come. When she had read *Victory* she kept asking: Why did they have to come? Why couldn't they get lost on the way? But she knew the answer. The forces of evil and darkness always get there in the end. You always have to fight them in the end. No matter how canny you are, or how careful not to tell anyone where you're going, or how scrupulous about covering your tracks, it's no good. They always turn up anyway. Sometimes there are moments when you think you've lost them, but they've just let you get a little ahead for a while.

She walked slowly around the gardens in the long dying gloom of the twilight, listening to her heart slow down to its normal pulse. She followed the same paths winding between the box hedges and the yew hedges, and her heels clicked along the cobbled walks that went under the stone archways to the stable yard. She wandered through the kitchen garden with its neat rows of beans and cabbages and into the long arbor with its trellises of roses and borders of zinnias and pansies.

At the end of the gardens the flight of stone steps led to the water. She picked her way down them and sat on the last step, leaning against the slab of stone at the bottom. When she had been here before, she had seen fish below the river's surface: a school of fingerlings darting back and forth and two trout swaying lazily in the current as they slowly drifted upstream. Now in the darkness the surface of the water was black and mysterious, throwing back the fading reflection of the trees along the bank. The river looked opaque and sinister as it wound past her feet, and the shadows in the trees moved in a threatening and unfriendly rhythm. She sat as still as she could, hoping that stillness would make her safe, that stillness would keep them from noticing her.

Discouragement enveloped her fear. She would never be able to get along with anyone. When she and Sam had been friends, she couldn't leave well enough alone. Now that she knew she wanted him she had lost him. Wasn't it always like that? Yes. That was the answer. Yes. That was how they arranged it. She slumped down on the stones and gazed thoughtlessly out at the water.

She must have dozed off, or gone back into places in her mind so deep that being there was almost like sleep, because the noise of Travis scrambling down the stone steps behind her made her jump with a sharp, scared intake of breath. He sat down next to her on the step, dispelling the ghosts with his healthy presence.

"Hi. What are you doing, hiding out? I sure had enough trouble finding you." He picked up a chip of stone and heaved it into the water. The splash broke the surface, and a fish jumped in the concentric waves that formed around it. The river was just water again.

"Guess what?" he said. "Guess what he did after you left the dining room?"

"What."

"He kicked me right out of here, that's what. Just ordered me to go off and see the rest of Europe as of right now. 'I think the time has come for us to go our separate ways, Travis,' " Travis mimicked his father. Another stone crashed into the surface of the river. "What do you think of that?"

"So when do you plan to go?"

"Tomorrow, I guess, although I got the impression to-night wouldn't be too soon for him. Boy, what a sorehead. I guess he figured out about us and he just can't take it. It's not like you two are married or something. I mean, I can't help it if you have a crush on me, what am I supposed to do about it?" He looped his arm over her shoulder and drew her toward him, letting his hand rest proprietarily on her breast and giving it an absentminded squeeze through her sweater.

She carefully moved his hand and shrugged her shoulders out from under his arm. "What makes you think I had a crush on you?" she said.

"What's the matter? Look at how you came on to me this afternoon—you aren't denying what happened, are you?" He looped his arm back across her shoulders. She shrugged it off.

"Maybe we misunderstood each other," she said.

"Oh, come on, you don't have to be so embarrassed about it, it was just a crush."

"What makes you so sure of it? I mean, when did you start thinking I felt that way?"

"Well, I don't know exactly. I always thought you were pretty sexy, right from the beginning. But at first we didn't get along too well. You were uptight about something."

"That's right."

"Anyway, when Jake left, he mentioned that he thought you would go with him, and then you didn't."

"What made you think it was because of you?"

"Just instinct, I guess. But remember that night we all went fishing after Jake left? I think it was after Jake left. There was a big storm?"

"Yes, it was after Jake left."

"Okay, so anyway, I came up behind you to see if you had any extra leader I could borrow. Remember that?"

"I didn't know what you wanted."

"You looked so terrified and tiny all alone out there in that storm."

"So?"

"I don't know." He shrugged. "After that was when I realized that Dad wasn't really taking care of you. And you got interested in me too."

"I *was* interested."

"Well, you certainly showed it. All those questions. And today when you reached over and started playing with my wrist, that was certainly a major come-on. You can't deny what happened then. You wanted it, too. You wanted it bad." He drew out the last word. "I don't know what's going on with you and Dad, but you sure liked getting a proper fucking." He grinned over at her in the half-light and looped his arm back over her shoulders, leaning forward with his other hand on her thigh. "Didn't you?"

"I guess there's been a lot of misunderstanding." She moved away, ducking out from under his arm.

"Okay, okay, your feelings have changed. Have it your way, I don't care." Travis looked glumly out at the river.

"Where do you think you'll go next?" she asked after a while.

"I don't know. I guess I'll go back to Mom's for a while. At least I'm welcome there. I'm certainly not going to drag ass around Europe just because Dad thinks it would be good for me. I only came here to see him."

"You might enjoy traveling some more if you weren't so angry about all this."

"Listen, as far as I'm concerned this whole situation is nuts and I'm going to get as far away from it as I can. First you're the juiciest little piece who has wanted me in a long time, then all of a sudden I'm not even allowed to kiss you. First Dad writes me this letter bringing me halfway around the fucking world for this great reunion or something, and now it turns out he doesn't ever want to see me again. You're both crazy. Some father he turned out to be." Travis's voice resonated with cold, disgusted anger.

"It wasn't all his fault."

"Oh, right, the butler did it."

"It would be awful if this meeting made you like each other even less. That certainly wasn't the intention." She stopped herself from saying "my intention."

"Come on, that's the way he's always been. Stupid and stuck-up and angry at me. I guess I just needed reminding."

"Listen, it really wasn't Sam's idea to bring you over here," she said.

"Whose was it, then?"

"Well, he did it, but it started when I first heard about you. It seemed to me that it was bad for Sam not to see you. I could tell he was more upset about it than he knew himself. And it looked like you had gotten kind of a bad deal."

"Very perceptive."

"Anyway, I guess I sort of nagged him into asking you here, or at least into doing something about you."

"Good work."

"It just didn't seem right that he had a son he had abandoned like that. It didn't fit with the way I wanted him to be."

"What made it your business?"

"Just that I cared about Sam."

"You cared so much about him that you couldn't just leave well enough alone, is that it?"

"I guess so." She was sorry.

"And Jake, I always wondered why he sicced that drip Jake on me. I bet that was another one of your brilliant ideas, right?"

"I just wanted the four of us to have a good time together. I thought maybe it would be easier for Sam to ask you if there was someone your own age to travel with." She shrugged in despair. "I don't know. It seemed to make sense at the time."

"Very convenient, very neat. I don't suppose it occurred to you that Jake and I aren't exactly well suited to be friends."

"I guess we didn't think about that. I'm really sorry, Travis. There have been a lot of mistakes. I am sorry."

Travis stood up, dislodging a small slide of stones which tumbled down the bank into the water. He looked down at her in the darkness as if he wanted to kill her. Now he had a reason to. She pressed back against the stones. Whatever happened, she deserved it. But instead of moving toward her, Travis headed up the steps, taking them in two strides. He stopped at the top and turned back.

"You guys are supposed to be so smart," he said, his voice level and cool now. "You guys are supposed to be so damn smart. Please, after this, could you just leave me alone?"

The last she saw of him was his broad, unyielding back, disappearing over the edge of the steps, into the darkness.

Chapter

25

Night had fallen by the time she started back to the castle alone. She climbed up the steps and walked through the gardens. In the darkness everything looked different, and as she followed a gravel path next to a brick wall somewhere on the other side of the vegetable gardens she realized that she had lost her way. Stifling her panic, she doubled back until she reached the familiar shape of the rose trellis. All right. It was going to be all right.

This time she turned through another archway and found herself on the driveway below the castle. Now she began to worry about being late. What if they locked the door? What if she couldn't get inside? Her heart raced as she ran up the gravel sweep and tried the big brass knob. It turned and the door swung open under her hand. She stood against the wall, panting, while the ghosts and ghouls of the night swirled in frustration outside.

Up the stairs. The sooner she got to the bedroom, the less suspicious Sam would be. She pushed away the logical conclusion that Sam had sent Travis away because he already knew. How was she going to deal with Sam? Could she convince him that nothing had happened, that what had happened wasn't important, that what was important wasn't what had happened? Under pressure, her mind clogged and stalled. All she wanted was for Sam to forgive her and comfort her. Sam, her friend Sam. She slowly opened the door to the bedroom.

Her friend Sam was sound asleep, snoring softly into a mound of pillows, with his arms around them. He was wearing his pajamas. The lights were on. A half-empty bottle of whiskey stood next to an empty glass on the bedside table and the Gingrich book lay on its face among the tangled covers. Looking beyond the bed, she saw that he had taken his suitcase out of the closet and laid it on the luggage rack. A few pairs of socks and underpants were neatly folded in the bottom, but something had apparently interrupted his methodical packing. Drawers were left open in uncharacteristic disarray, and Travis's blue sweater bulged out from the bottom of the bureau where she had stuffed it earlier in the evening.

She crossed the room to wake him up. But standing above his boyish, sleeping form, she stopped herself. What good would it do to talk to him now? He was tired and probably drunk. She was cringing and wanted reassurance. If she was going to get him back, she would have to learn to leave him alone. The reason for waking him was to prove she wasn't out with Travis. What better proof could there be than having her here beside him, asleep, when he woke up on his own?

Gently, trying not to make any noise, she turned off the bedside light. She was a solicitous mother looking down on her slumbering boy. Lullaby and good night. Quietly, she refolded the clothes on the chair and shut the drawers, returning the room to its normal order. She put the bottle of whiskey in the closet and rinsed out the glass in the bathroom across the hall. Then she undressed, turned out the other lamp, and slipped into bed next to Sam. She put the book on the table and straightened the sheets around him. He turned away in his sleep and lay on his side, breathing heavily.

Hannah lay in the dark and tried to sleep. The events of the day kept replaying themselves in her mind. If only she hadn't touched Travis's wrist. If only it had been raining. Down the hall she heard a door shut. Was it Travis, preparing to leave? If only he had never come. If only she had minded her own business and appreciated Sam for what he was instead of wanting him to be what he wasn't—a man who could deal with a difficult son. In a shallow doze, she relived and regretted the events of the last two weeks. Slowly she slid deeper into the cottony blur of unconsciousness.

In her dream she and Sam and Travis were all staying at the Ritz in Boston. The swan boats were out in the Public Gardens and there were blossoms on the trees along Commonwealth Avenue. Sam had gone out and while he was gone she and Travis had gotten into bed. They were just playing. Playing between the crisp white sheets with the pink counterpane. When Sam came back, she was terrified that he would find out. Suddenly he seemed clean and strong and golden. Travis, behind her, was dirty and unkempt. Worse, she couldn't control him. When Sam turned his back, he tried to catch her eye with a knowing, lecherous grin. When Sam was on the telephone, he puckered up his lips and made leering, kissing sounds toward her, like the men in the dining room. She signaled her disapproval with a frown, but he kept it up. He was laughing at her.

When she woke up, Sam was already dressed. She had overslept and missed the comforting clipping and splashing sounds of his morning rituals. He was leaning over the open suitcase, neatly placing the last of his folded shirts on the top. She rolled over toward him and propped herself up on one arm. The squeak of the bedsprings startled him and he turned around.

"Oh, good morning," he said. His tone was polite, even friendly, but his eyes were blank.

"Hi, Sam," she said. He looked wonderful. Tanned and handsome, with a deep-cobalt-blue turtleneck under his blue oxford shirt. She loved him a lot at that moment. She would love him until he loved her back.

"Are we leaving?" she said.

"Yes." Sam spoke while he finished packing and tied the silk inner straps of his suitcase into their tiny brass buckles. "I've been down already. Travis has apparently left. That's just as well, he has plenty of cash and his tickets home. If we leave sometime this morning, we can probably get to Shannon tomorrow. Anyway, I've made reservations back to New York on Aer Lingus in case we do."

Sam was all business. He sounded as if he was talking to a faithful servant or a casual traveling companion.

"I guess I'd better get a move on," she said.

"I guess so." He closed his suitcase. "I'll go down and take care of the bill. Maybe we can get some coffee before we go."

At least he still said "we." She got up and wrapped herself in her trench coat. Something about Sam's tone this morning made her feel embarrassed to be naked in front of him. She crossed the hall to the bathroom and took a bath, packing shampoo and soap and toothpaste as she used them. She could be efficient, too. By the time she got back to the bedroom, Sam and his suitcase were gone. She dressed and packed as fast as she could, folding her shirts and sweaters in the air and stuffing her socks and underwear in at the last minute instead of rolling them up inside her boots. She had to put the suitcase on the floor and sit on it to close it. It was a good thing Sam wasn't around to disapprove. She left Travis's blue sweater behind in the bottom drawer of the bureau.

Sam was downstairs in the parlor waiting for her. He managed to adopt a manner of waiting which was superior without being impatient. It wasn't that he didn't have something else to do—he was sipping his coffee and reading the paper. It was just that it was time to leave. When she came into the room he stood up. She reached for a cup of coffee and hurriedly gulped at it, burning her tongue in the process.

"Don't hurry, you'll just burn yourself," Sam said. He picked up her bag and headed outdoors. It was another beautiful day. She laid her trench coat in the back seat as Sam put the suitcases in the trunk. Carefully she unbuttoned her shirt cuffs and folded back the sleeves for summer. Then she fished her sunglasses out of her canvas bag and perched them on top of her head. For a moment she felt glamorous and confident. Her reflection in the car window before she opened the door reminded her how attractive she was. But beyond her own face through the glass she saw Sam's tense profile, upright in the driver's seat, waiting for her.

He drove fast. Letterkenny, Stranorlar, Ballybofey, and on through Donegal without stopping. At lunchtime he pulled over at a roadside pub and they bought some sandwiches to eat in the car. Pre-cut, with dried-out bread and ham turning up at the corners. Ballintra, Ballyshannon, Tullaghan, Mullaghmore, Cliffony. The long bay of Donegal stretched out behind them and the distinctive square shape of Ben Bulben hunkered off to the side again. Sligo, Collooney, Tobercurry. Driving back at this speed made Ireland seem small. How few miles separated place from place. As they raced through the little towns, between the high hedgerows or over the flat brown bogs, she had a kind of vertigo. It was as if they were reliving the trip backward, at high speeds, like a home movie on fast rewind.

They hardly talked. Sam seemed wholly intent on getting there, but as they drove she tried to decipher his silences. He didn't seem angry. How much did he understand of what had gone on? How much did he hold her responsible for? At times his face looked nervous and tight and his jaw muscles clenched and unclenched just under the skin. Other times he looked terribly sad. Once, at a stop sign for a crossroads in the middle of nowhere, he seemed to lose track of himself completely. She looked over when the car had been stopped longer than usual and saw him gazing in a dazed way out at the bogs. His mouth drooped and his eyes seemed to sag in the center; his whole face looked dragged down by some awful inner sorrow.

"Sam?" He snapped back to his businesslike self and accelerated out of the crossroads with a roar.

It was afternoon by the time they got to Charlestown. Sam stopped the car on a shoulder and pulled the map out of the glove compartment.

"I don't think we're going to make it much farther south tonight," he said, unfolding the map. "We may as well stop."

"Okay." Time was on her side.

"There's a good hotel near Westport I've heard about," he said. "We'll go over there and try to get an early start in the morning."

"Sounds fine."

Sam opened the guide and took the map of County Mayo out of the book's back pocket. "There are a couple of things we should see down here if we have time," he said. "Croagh Patrick, which is supposed to be the sacred mountain where Saint Patrick banished the snakes from Ireland, and Rockfleet Castle, where Granny Wales, the female pirate, lived."

"That sounds interesting," she said. Stay quiet, don't pressure him, don't blow his willingness to talk. "Saint Patrick banished the snakes?"

"Well, that's the legend. There aren't any snakes in Ireland and the story is that he banished them." Sam shrugged. "Who knows, the distinction between myth and history is pretty murky here."

"I wonder if there's some biological explanation for it," she said. "The no snakes, I mean." The green-eyed monster jealousy, the dark serpent of sex.

This time he didn't answer. He carefully folded and replaced the map and they turned toward Swinford and Castlebar on the N 5. The road into Westport ran flat through bogs and fields of stubble edged by damp haystacks. The farmers held them together with crisscrossings of rope that made it look as if the stacks were wearing hair nets. They drove into town over a small river and past a tiny village green with a statue at its center. Sam stopped at the green and let the car idle, searching the crannies of his mind for the name of the good hotel near Westport.

"Newport! That's it." He turned north toward an arrow on a signpost. "I think the place is called Newport House."

"How did you hear about it?"

"You know, I don't even remember. Someone recommended it to me, maybe at the office, or the club."

The land between the two towns was so flat along the coast that it was hard to find the dividing line between the green mossy rocks and the opaque green water. Out in Clew Bay, the surface of the sea was dotted with dozens of low islands, and the road bridged stream after stream opening out into this latticework of earth and ocean.

"There it is," Sam said. As they approached the cluster of gray stone buildings at the corner of the bay, he turned toward a sign for Newport House. Almost immediately they turned again through an elaborate wrought-iron arch and across groomed green lawns spreading in the shade of ancient trees. Sam stopped the car in front of the stone steps up to the door. A man came out to help with the bags and soon they were being shown to a spacious room painted in pale-blue with Wedgwood-white moldings.

Newport House was very different from Ballymarr, but it was also exactly the same. It was a house instead of a castle. And it had the feeling of being a house, with echoes of children playing with hoops on the lawn—and being scolded by Nanny for running in the halls. There was nothing imposing or spooky about the friendly trees and gardens or the narrow hallways hung with hunting prints. And the bright front rooms still sustained the cozy air of Victorian family life.

Still, as Hannah stepped into the hall she felt an odd click of recognition, a tingling in her blood. There was an almost perceptible low humming sound in the air—a hum which came from everything being done in the proper way that things should be done. The hum of human comfort being attended to with grace and elegance. It had something to do with the freshness of the linens and the paisley-patterned curtains and coverlets in their room, and something to do with the impeccable grounds, and something to do with the fresh flowers at the reception desk. But it was more than the sum of all of these parts. Now as she tried to analyze the sound, the feeling, she remembered it at Ballymarr too, and once when Sam had taken her for a drink at the Century Club in the wood-paneled room on the second floor, and once, a long time ago, when a school friend of her father's had had them for a weekend on his private boat on Lake Michigan.

How did Sam find these places? They didn't have special designations in the guidebook, yet he had zeroed in on Newport House like a homing pigeon. He heard about them, from friends or colleagues or family. And he remembered. There would be something in the tone of a man's voice, or something he said that seemed incidental at the time, which clued in his colleagues and clubmates. A slight lowering of the eyes or a minute shift in accent would signify that, yes, Newport House was one of those places. You know, nice hotels, for people like us. When people-like-us traveled, they moved in a world as isolated and as pleasant as the well-worn routes from their corner offices to their clubs and their upper-East-Side co-ops. They had a kind of underground railroad of spaciousness and comfort and needs-well-attended. And in fact, the places they stayed in were often less expensive than the impersonal big chain tourist hotels they abhorred. It wasn't entirely a matter of money.

Hannah understood all this, and she valued it. Sam's way of life made starving in a garret seem silly instead of romantic. It was no fun having to clean your own floors, and waiting in line all the time for almost everything, and not being able to get away for some quiet time even when you desperately needed it.

Now, in the pink-and-red light cast by the beginning of the sunset, they turned back out through the wrought-iron archway and drove toward Rockfleet Castle. Sam had barely unpacked when he suggested the side trip.

"We might as well see something before dinner," he said. He was probably filling the time with activity so that he wouldn't have to think. Facing her over a drink would be too dangerous.

As they approached, they saw the square tower sticking abruptly out of the flats of Clew Bay. Its four stone sides rose precipitously out of the grass and rocks at the sea's edge, and they were pierced by an irregular pattern of weapon slits and one small arched door and window. The top of the tower was a peaked stone triangle, as if Rockfleet Castle was wearing Marianne Moore's tricorne hat.

"I like the idea of a woman pirate," she said.

"You would." They walked together over to a brass plaque bolted to the stones next to the arched doorway.

This tower house was once the residence of Granny Wales, or Grace O'Malley, known as the Pirate Queen. She beat off an English seaborne attack against the castle in 1570. Later Elizabeth I granted her permission to attack the Queen's enemies.

"Hey, look at that." The sun setting at the edge of Clew Bay made the islands shimmer in the light and the green of the water shift to beaten gold. The low cone of Croagh Patrick across from them turned red, and above it pink clouds and silver clouds floated puffy and weightless in long lines across the sky. They sat down on a flat stone at the edge of the castle to watch. She leaned her head against Sam's body, touching him for the first time.

"Oh, Sam," she said. "Let's be friends."

He didn't answer. She drew back her head and put her arms around his reluctant body.

"Yes?" she said. "No?" Sam looked steadfastly out at the spectacular sky as if he could see his future written in the puffs of cloud. She reached over and stroked the upper part of his chest with her hand, catching the edge of his shirt on the buckle of the watch she had been wearing since she took it from Travis. It looked out of place there. She should have taken it off.

"I see you got the watch back," Sam said.

"Sam, can't we just forget some things? I love being here with you, let's enjoy it. I want to be with you. I'm sorry."

More silence. From the side, she could see his jaw working. His whole body felt stiff and resistant, as if he were made of stone.

"Do you want to talk about it?" she said.

"I'm not sure I see any point in talking about it."

"You don't trust me, do you?"

"Have you given me any reason to?"

"No, maybe not, but I'm pleading with you not to be so angry, Sam. I'm sorry about what happened. There were reasons for it, but it was wrong and stupid. I know that. It doesn't have to be such a big deal."

"How can there be reasons for something like that?" He took her hand off his chest and let it drop next to her on the stones. She kept her other arm around him.

"Sam, you were pushing me away. I felt that I couldn't talk to you. You didn't *want* to know what was going on with me. I'm not trying to make excuses, but you just weren't there for me, you know? I was having a hard time and I had to hide everything from you because you didn't want to be bothered."

"I was trying to concentrate on Travis. You made me feel as if I was a lousy father. I was trying to change that."

"But you weren't paying much attention to him either."

"I don't know any more." Sam's body slumped down under her arm now. From the side she could see that his face was weighed down by sadness. "I don't know. I thought I had learned a lot from you. I tried to make everything come out all right, to go to the right sort of place and to be civilized about it and I guess it didn't work."

"Sam, you *have* learned a lot. It's just that sometimes you're very . . ." As she searched for the word she wanted, a word like *locked-up*, or *unbending*, or *rigid*, she felt the whole position of his body change. Suddenly he seemed softer to her touch and smaller. He leaned over and put his head in his hands, and his back jerked under her arm.

"Oh, God," he moaned. "I feel as if I've been so selfish. I feel as if I've lost so much." His voice came out in a low wail, and her heart went out to him.

"Come on, Sam, it's all right." She moved to cradle his head in her arms. He leaned against her and curled his legs up toward his stomach like a little boy, burying his head in her lap. Sam was crying.

"There, now, you're wonderful, Sam. I love you." She crooned and stroked his head, mother to his child.

"I just can't seem to connect with people. I thought I was different with you."

"You are different," she comforted him, "you are, you are." And he was. His body felt as if the starch had been taken out of it. He lay limp and sad and helpless in her arms.

It was getting darker now, the colors in the sky had faded to grays and deep blues. They had probably missed dinner, and Sam hadn't even noticed. The stone they were sitting on began to turn chilly as they sat there almost motionless in the end of the long day, a woman cuddling and murmuring to a man at the flat edge of Rockfleet Castle on Clew Bay on the west side of County Mayo on the last night of their visit to Ireland. Hannah looked over beyond the bay to the darkening green of the shadows at the foot of Croagh Patrick. One white horse walked slowly across the silent landscape to the sea.

Epilogue

Travis moved back into his old room on the second floor. His mother was happy to see him, at least. It was the beginning of August and he called a few friends from before he went west, but everyone was away for the summer. He didn't mind. The days passed pleasantly enough. He did chores around the house, weeding the dandelions out of the lawn and trimming the high privet hedge that separated it from the neat little sidewalk along Beechwood Road.

Other days he took the train into the city. It looked about the same. Noisy and crowded and dirty. One big change was the joggers he saw everywhere, even out in Ashmont. A lot of people wanted to tell him about their times and their distances. What a joke! Track was the one thing he was ever good at, but back then no one even knew about it. A lot of good it did him! Back then. Maybe he could show them a thing or two. One afternoon he drove over to Mount Kisco and bought the works. Shorts, tank top, and a bright pair of Brooks Vantage Supremes.

He had figured to give it a try, at least. But he was at

home right away, just swinging along to the rhythmic slapping of his shoes on the asphalt and the sounds of his own heavy breathing. When he ran, his mind emptied out and filled up again with thoughts about his body, or the scenery, or the next mile. The problem of what he was going to do with his life seemed unimportant. It would all work out somehow. In the meantime, what he was going to do was run.

He started off each morning with stretches on the front lawn, and then he would lope off down Beechwood and the intersecting tree-shaded streets. Birch Road and Ash Drive and Allegheny Lane. He ran over bridges and through underpasses, down Route 117 and over 9A and on into the Greenburgh hills. He ran through the dirt roads of Bedford, with its grand houses set back behind big oaks, and past the white paddock fences of North Salem, and through rows of new houses with streets named Doris and Tina and Gloria after the developers' wives and daughters.

After Labor Day his mother drove him up to the Bob Howes Memorial ten-mile race in Connecticut, and he was hooked. He came to crave the feeling of tension and expectation at the start of a race, and he loved the people who cheered and clapped along the route and went wild at the finish line. They were cheering for him! They were clapping for him! He raced through the streets of Greenwich, where horsy girls with long straight hair passed out Gatorade as the runners passed, and he raced through Italian neighborhoods where big fat Mommas passed out water and almond candies, and through the industrial plazas along Route 1, where the workers came out of their factories and showrooms to cheer the runners on.

At every race he made friends, and they compared notes on times and traffic and which routes were safe from dogs. He bought every book he could find and at night he spent hours combing through Kenneth Cooper and George Sheehan and Bill Rodgers's marathoning book for information and help. He read Jim Fixx's big red book cover to cover—it was the first time he could remember being that interested in a book. He needed to know. At first when he picked up a paperback of *The Loneliness of the Long-Distance Runner* at the bookstore, he thought he had made a mistake. But then when he started skipping around in it, it began to look pretty interesting. "It was hard to understand and all I knew was that you had to run, run, run . . ." he read. Then he started at the beginning and finished the story. It was slow going. Often he had to go over a sentence two or three times. But it was worth it. He could really understand that guy and his running and the angry way he felt.

Travis was fast. He pushed himself harder, farther, every day, reaching for that wonderful high after a run at the edge of his endurance, his whole body hot, his legs gently aching, and his head about a mile off the ground. His legs hardened and veins and sinews pushed out through the skin; his face took on weathered hollows. At the end of October he began training seriously for the Jersey Shore marathon. He didn't want to tell anyone, because that would make it not happen, but he thought maybe he could run it in under three hours. That would qualify him for Boston in April. And Boston was the Mecca of runners, the top, the race that everyone dreamed about. He could try, at least. He concentrated on training, blocking out everything else.

Late summer had turned to autumn and he ran about seventy miles a week, through the Hudson Valley orchards, rich with the tangy smell of apples, and over piles of red and golden leaves at the side of the road. The earth smelled like the end of summer, but every now and then a blast of fresh wind tasted like the snow. There were fading marigolds in the gardens he passed and pumpkins in the farms above

Croton. Sometimes he'd run along with the school bus; he'd wave at the kids coming home with their empty lunch boxes and their grins of daily liberation.

One of the nicest things was that his Mom was so enthusiastic about it. It gave her something to do for him and they got along wonderfully. She studied up on nutrition for athletes and bought him clothes and even kept his log sometimes. He didn't let her down. And there was always a lot to talk about. A couple of times she asked him about Sam and his new girl friend, especially after the engagement was announced. But he finessed it. He knew that hearing about them would just make her feel bad, and he didn't want that.

The air inside the Asbury Park convention hall before the Jersey Shore marathon was like electricity. Everyone was doing stretches or cameling up with water before the start. Travis paced himself carefully. Down to Long Branch and back to Asbury, down and back. He remembered how Jim Fixx says to start out slowly. And he thought of how Alan Sillitoe wrote about never being in a hurry during a race, and especially about never letting anyone see you're in a hurry. It was cold but his body felt warm and even-temperatured like a machine working in perfect sync. After the tenth mile he got a stitch—a searing pain across the left side of his torso. But he breathed in and out, exhaling as hard as he could and bellying out his gut with each breath. He had read about it and he knew what to do. The running took over and the ache receded. Time seemed endless. Run, run, run. At the finish line there were crowds and the roar of cheering and the grit of one last push. Through a salty haze of pain he focused on the big digital clock. 2:56:33, it said. He was going to Boston.

It was late winter now, and he ran through the naked January landscape. After a storm he ran along the top of the snow at the edge of the road; it was warmer and softer than the frozen asphalt. The air tingled against his skin as his body warmed up in the icy weather. He was glowing with warmth and power while ordinary people hurried along miserably all bundled up and hunched over against the cold. He ran by them smiling, heated from inside by his own hot blood. The heart, the runner's inner source.

He took the bus from downtown Boston out to Hopkinton with the other runners, leaving his extra clothes at the Prudential Center. He wore his blue Jersey Shore T-shirt and he jammed his red woolen hat down over his head. He knew he would want to take it off during the race, but he needed it for the cold start. This was as good a place to lose it as any. Afterward he would buy a new hat.

At the start, the top guys, the celebrities like Bill Rodgers and Frank Shorter, lined up ahead of the mob. He had never seen so many people on one level at the same time before. It was a cool, drizzly day and he filled his lungs with the damp April air. He was ready. Sandwiched into the crowd, he felt bouncy and light. He heard the starting gun go off somewhere ahead of him. No one moved. Finally they began to walk. He broke into a slow run, but the crush slowed him back down to a walk. It was eight minutes into the race when Travis crossed the starting line, and another fifty seconds before he was able to start running at a steady pace. He'd just have to make it up. He ran steadily and slowly, keeping his impatience under control. After the first five miles he fell in with another runner. *Seattle Striders,* his red T-shirt said.

"Rotten start."

"We'll make it up." But he hadn't begun to. They passed two women runners and a man running in a tuxedo and ruffled dress shirt.

"I hope it's rented," the Strider said. He picked up his pace and Travis watched as the red shirt slowly edged ahead and vanished in the throng in front of him. It was too early to push. The crowd was beginning to thin and Travis ran alone. The sound of his feet on the pavement hypnotized him. He couldn't imagine not running. Time slowed down to a walk. He thought about his father and Hannah. He had seen their engagement announcement in *The Times* but he hadn't heard from either of them. Not that he expected to. He imagined Hannah with her round face enclosed in a scratchy white lace veil. Jake would be at her side in a frock coat, looking uncomfortable as he always did. Sam would stand on the other side—old enough to be the father of the bride. A bunch of penguins.

Dearly beloved, we are gathered together here . . .

He was so, so glad that he wasn't going to be gathered together there, in front of the tinsely altar of St. Bart's, in a new tight suit that made him sweat like a fool. Oh, no, he wasn't the tame son Sam wanted. The son who would smile and agree how beautiful the bride was, how lucky the groom.

No, he was wild and he always had been. Wild and sweet, wild and free, swinging along in this noble pack of men and women, a string of bright colors stretching like a human ribbon from Framingham to Commonwealth Avenue in the spring day. People were cheering all along the way. After Wellesley he took off his hat and tossed it to a pretty blonde girl in the crowd. She caught it and smiled.

At Heartbreak Hill a man was spraying the runners with a hose. By now Travis's body was so hot he expected the water to sizzle off his skin like drops in a frying pan. That was when he knew he wasn't going to cramp up or hit the wall or anything like that. That was when he knew he was going to make it.

His mom was at the beginning of Commonwealth Avenue, cheering along with a crowd of other parents and friends. Sometimes she looked like a brittle suburban lady, but now she had smiles in her eyes.

"You're looking great!" she called. He passed a runner who was limping painfully along the curb. Another man sat doubled over in pain at the side, with a friend bent over him in concern. He heard the wail of an ambulance behind him. But he was okay. The roar of the crowd vibrated somewhere inside his head.

"Way to go!" they yelled.

"Keep it up, Jersey Shore!"

"Way to go, Jersey Shore!" That was him! They were cheering for him! Everyone was with him now, everyone was on his side. Ahead, he saw the great square shape of the Prudential Tower. He was making it! Oh, he was so fast, he was a man, a *mensch,* a winner. His body was wet and sore but his mind spun with victory. Down Commonwealth Avenue with the crowd going wild. Around the corner and uphill, running beside another man in blue. Too hurting to feel happy any more, falling over his own feet, with his head flying about a mile above his body. Over the last rise and to the left and down to the finish. 3:05:24. He hadn't made up his slow start, but he didn't care. The other man in the blue T-shirt embraced him.

"We made it," he sobbed, "we made it." They walked into the chutes to register. Lined up with their hands on each other's shoulders like an elephant train. It was hard to move. Travis gave his number and someone handed him a silver Mylar cape to wrap around his shoulders. He was shivering now. They were all wandering around in these silver capes like angels.

"Hi, Travis," a voice behind him said. "How did you do?" It was one of the other runners who had qualified at Jersey

Shore. Travis tried to grin but his mouth was sore and his gums felt like cotton.

"Not so great, I guess, three-oh-five, but I feel like I won the bastard," he got out.

"I know what you mean. Is your mom here? I thought I saw her on that last stretch."

Smiling was getting easier now. "Yeah, that was her. I hope she cheered you on."

"Sure did. She's great. My whole family's here, they love it. How come your dad never comes to these things?"

Travis looked over at the friendly face, the friendly innocent face. He loved this guy. Maybe he would never see him again, but he loved him. They were brothers. For this moment, they were brothers.

"Oh, my dad took off years ago," Travis said. He shrugged his silver shoulders to show that he didn't mind any more. "I haven't seen him since I was a kid."

ABOUT THE AUTHOR

Susan Cheever's first novel, *Looking for Work,*
was published in 1979. Born in New York
City in 1943, Ms. Cheever graduated from
Brown University. She has also been a teacher,
a reporter for the *Tarrytown Daily News,* a free-
lance journalist, and a writer for *Newsweek*
magazine.